Please renew or retur
shown on your receip

D0475787

www.hertsdirect.org

Renewals and enquiries: 0300 123 4049

Textphone for hearing or 0300 123 4041
speech impaired users:

L32

COSMOS

*By the same author
and available from MacGibbon & Kee*

*

FERDYDURKE

WITOLD GOMBROWICZ

COSMOS

English version by
ERIC MOSBACHER

MACGIBBON & KEE

FIRST PUBLISHED 1965 IN POLISH BY
THE INSTYTUT LITERACKI (KULTURA) PARIS
FIRST PUBLISHED 1967 IN ENGLISH BY
MACGIBBON & KEE LIMITED
3 UPPER JAMES STREET
GOLDEN SQUARE LONDON W1
COPYRIGHT © WITOLD GOMBROWICZ 1965
ENGLISH TRANSLATION COPYRIGHT © 1967
BY MACGIBBON & KEE LIMITED
PRINTED IN GREAT BRITAIN BY
CLARKE, DOBLE & BRENDON LTD
CATTEDOWN, PLYMOUTH

NOTE

Title of the Polish original *Kosmos*. This version by Eric Mosbacher made from the French translation by Georges Sedir and the German translation (*Indizien*) by Walter Tiel.

COSMOS

I

BUT let me tell you about another, even more curious adventure.

It was sweltering. Fuchs tramped on ahead and I followed behind. Trouser-legs. Heels. Sand. On we plodded. Earth. Ruts. The road was vile. Gleams from shiny pebbles, the air shimmering and buzzing with heat, everything black with sunlight. Houses, fences, fields and woods. What a road. What a tramp. Where we were coming from and why . . . but that would be a long story. The fact of the matter was that I was sick of my parents, and indeed the whole family, and also I wanted to pass at least one exam and get right away from it all. So I took off to Zakopane and was walking through Krupowki, wondering where to find a good cheap pension, when whom should I run into but Fuchs. Fuchs had carroty hair, fading into blond, and dead, protruding, fish-like eyes, but he was pleased to see me and I was pleased to see him, how are you, what are you doing here, I'm looking for a room, so am I, I've got an address (he said), a little place right out in the country where it's cheaper because it's a long way out, right outside the village. So off we went. Trouser-legs, heels in the sand, the road, the heat. I stared at my feet. Earth and sand, glistening pebbles, one foot after the other, trouser-legs, heels, sweat, my eyes kept blinking with fatigue, I had slept badly in the train, and on we plodded in the sweltering heat. There was nothing but this endless, ground-level plodding.

He stopped.

'Shall we stop and have a rest?'

'How far do we still have to go?'

'Not very far now'.

I looked round at what was to be seen, though I had no desire to see it, because I had seen it so often already—pines and hedges, firs and houses, grass and weeds, a ditch, foot-paths and flower-beds, fields and a chimney. The air was

9

shimmering with sunlight, but black, the trees were black, the earth was grey, the vegetation at ground-level was green, but everything was pretty black. A dog barked. Fuchs strode off towards a roadside thicket.

'It'll be cooler,' he said.

'No, let's go on.'

'Let's have a short rest first.'

He plunged deeper into the thicket, where there were shady nooks and corners under the mingling branches of hazel-trees and pines. I gazed into the maze of leaves and branches, dappled light, dense vegetation, gaps and recesses and windings and slopes and yawning chasms and heaven knows what else besides that advanced on us and receded, forced us aside and yielded to us, jostled us and made way for us. . . . Lost and dripping with sweat, I felt the bare, black earth under my feet. But there, among the branches, was something peculiar and strange, though at first I could not make out exactly what it was. My companion had seen it and was staring at it too.

'It's a sparrow.'

'Good heavens alive.'

Yes, it was a sparrow. A sparrow hanging from a bit of wire. It had been hanged. Its little head was bent and its mouth wide open. It was hanging by a bit of wire attached to a branch of a tree.

Extraordinary. A hanged bird. A hanged sparrow. This shrieking eccentricity indicated that a human hand had penetrated this fastness. Who on earth could have done such a thing, and why? I wondered, standing in the midst of this chaos, this proliferating vegetation with its endless complications, my head full of the rattle and clatter of the night-long train journey, insufficient sleep, the air and the sun and the tramp through the heat with this man Fuchs, and Jesia and my mother, the row about the letter and my rudeness to the old man, and Julius, and also Fuchs's troubles with his chief at the office (about which he had told me), and the bad road, and the ruts and lumps of earth and heels, trouser-legs, stones, and all this vegetation, all culminating like a crowd genuflecting before this hanged sparrow—reigning triumphant and eccentric over this outlandish spot.

'Who on earth could have done a thing like that?'
"Some boy or other.'
'No, it's too high.'
'Let's go.'

But he didn't budge. The sparrow went on hanging. Except for some grassy patches, the earth was bare. A lot of things were lying about: a strip of galvanised iron, a twig, another twig, a torn cardboard box, a broken off branch. There were also a beetle and an ant, and another ant, an unknown worm, a log, and so on and so forth, all the way to the undergrowth at the foot of the trees. He stared at all this, just as I did. 'Let's go,' he said, but he stayed where he was and went on staring, and the sparrow went on hanging, and I stayed there and went on staring too. 'Come on,' he said, but we didn't move, perhaps because we had already stayed there too long and had missed the right moment for going, and now, with that sparrow hanging in the trees, the situation grew graver and more unmanageable every moment, and I had the feeling that there was something disproportionate, untactful or unmannerly about us. I was sleepy.

'Come on,' I said, and off we went, leaving the sparrow in the trees behind us, alone.

But plodding on down that road in the heat of the sun made us sweat again, it was too much, and after going a short way we stopped, exhausted and miserable, and again I asked if we still had a long way to go. Fuchs replied by pointing to a notice on a fence.

'Look,' he said, 'they've got rooms to let there.'

I looked. Behind the fence there was a garden, and a sad, cheap, tedious house, lacking in ornamentation and balconies, with a gimcrack flight of steps leading up to the front door. It was built of wood in the Zakopane fashion, with two rows of windows, five on the ground floor and five on the first floor. As for the garden, there were some dwarf trees, and some pansies withering in the flower-beds, and some gravel paths. But Fuchs was in favour of trying the place, we had nothing to lose, after all, sometimes in joints like that the cooking was first class, he said, and also it might be very cheap. I too was willing to go in and see what the place was like, though we had previously walked past several houses with rooms to let without taking any notice of them. But it was sweltering, and the sweat was pouring from us. Fuchs opened the little gate, and we walked up the gravel path towards the shining window-panes. He rang the bell, we waited for a few moments on the top step, the door opened, and a woman appeared. She was past her first youth, about forty, perhaps, she was buxom, and seemed to be the maid.

'We should like to see the rooms you have to let.'

'Just a moment, please, I'll go and fetch madam.'

We waited on the top step, my head was still buzzing with the journey, the clatter of the train, the events of the day before, the crowds, the fumes, the din. The noise in my head was deafening. I was startled by a strange deformity in the decent, domesticated, blue-eyed face of the woman who opened the door. Her mouth seemed to be excessively prolonged to one side, though only to an infinitesmal extent, perhaps about a millimetre, but when she spoke this imparted a darting or gliding, almost reptilian, motion to her upper lip. There was a repellent coldness, like that of a frog or snake, about those lateral movements of her mouth, but in spite of that the woman warmed and excited me, for there was a kind of obscure transition leading straight to her bed, to gliding, creeping sin. Also her voice surprised me. I don't know what I expected to come from that mouth of hers, but the voice with which she spoke was that of the ordinary, stoutish, middle-aged, domestic servant that she was. Next I heard it from inside the house.

'Aunt. Here are some gentlemen to see the rooms.'

A few moments later the individual so addressed advanced towards us on her short legs, as if on a roller. She was completely round. We exchanged a few phrases. Yes, certainly, a room for two with full pension, come this way please. There was a smell of freshly-ground coffee. A short corridor, a wooden staircase, a small landing. Will you be staying for long? I see, working for exams, it's very quiet indeed here, you'll be completely undisturbed. Upstairs another corridor and several doors, the house was small and poky. She opened the last door at the end of the corridor, and I saw at a glance the kind of room it was. Like all rooms to let, it was rather dark. The roller-blind was down, there were two beds and a wardrobe, a hat-stand, a jug on a tray, two bed-side lamps without bulbs and a mirror in an ugly, stained frame. A ray of sunlight coming in through the blind illuminated a patch of floor, and a smell of ivy and the buzzing of an insect also came in from outside. All the same there was a surprise, for one of the beds was occupied. A woman was lying on it, and I had the feeling that there was something slightly abnormal about the way she was doing so, though I had no idea what it was, whether it was because there was nothing on the bed but the mattress, or because one of her legs was lying on the metal springs, as the mattress had slipped a bit. At all events the combination of leg and metal springs struck me on that hot, buzzing, harassing day. Had she been asleep? When she saw us she sat up and tidied her hair.

'Lena, what are you doing, darling? . . . Let me introduce you to my daughter.'

She bowed her head in reply to our greeting, got up, and walked out. Her silence made me forget the idea that something unusual had been going on here.

We were also shown the neighbouring room, which was similar but a little cheaper, because it did not have direct access to the bathroom. Fuchs sat on the bed, Mrs Wojtys sat on a small chair, and the result was that we took this cheaper room, with full board. In regard to the cooking, Mrs Wojtys said: 'Gentlemen, you will see for yourselves.' It was arranged that we should have breakfast and lunch in our room and dinner with the family downstairs.

'Fetch your things and Katasia and I will get the room ready.'

We went down and collected our things and then we came back with them.

We unpacked, and Fuchs expressed his satisfaction. The room was cheap, the place he had been recommended would certainly have been dearer, besides which it was much farther out. And we were going to be fed like turkey-cocks, just you wait and see.

I was getting more and more tired of his fish-face, and all

I wanted was sleep. I went over to the window and looked out. The miserable little garden lay stewing in the hot sunshine, and on the other side of the fence lay the road, and beyond it two pine-trees marked the spot where the sparrow was hanging in the thicket.

Feeling quite dizzy, I flung myself on the bed and dozed off. There was a mouth emerging from another mouth, there were lips with more lips round them, the lips were more like lips because they were less . . . but I fell fast asleep. Then I was awakened. The maid was standing over me.

It was early morning, a morning as black as night. No, it wasn't. 'Dinner's ready,' she said. I got up. Fuchs was already putting on his shoes. Dinner in the poky dining-room. Sideboard equipped with mirror. Yoghourt, radishes, and the eloquence of Mr Wojtys, a retired bank manager, complete with signet ring and gold cuff-links.

'Allow me to inform you, my dear sir, that I have now put myself entirely at the disposal of my better half and am now used by her for special services such as repairing the radio or fitting a new washer when a tap drips. Let me advise you, if I may be so bold, to take a little more butter with your radishes, the butter is first rate.'

'Thank you.'

'This heat will end in a thunderstorm, I'll be bound. In fact I'd be prepared to take a solemn oath on it by all that I consider most holy.'

'Didn't you hear the thunder in the distance behind the wood, papa?' (This was Lena, whom I hadn't seen properly yet, I couldn't really see anything at all distinctly, but at all events the retired bank manager had a picturesque way of expressing himself.)

'Why don't you have just a teeny-weeny bit more yoghourt? My wife is a quite outstanding specialist in the art of preparing yoghourt. And where do you suppose the secret lies, my dear sir? In the jug. The degree of perfection of the end-product in this case is directly related to the lactic qualities of the jug.'

'What do you know about it, Leo?' (This was an interruption by Mrs Wojtys.)

'I am a bridge player, gentlemen, a retired bank manager who by special permission of his wife now devotes himself every afternoon and on Sunday evenings to bridge. And so you two gentlemen are working for exams. Well, my humble abode is just the place for that, there's complete peace and quiet here, it's so quiet that you can go to sleep standing on your two legs, if I may be permitted to say so. . . .'

But I was hardly listening. Leo Wojtys was like a gnome. His head was like a gourd, and his bald pate, reinforced by the sarcastic flashing of his pince-nez, dominated the whole table. Lena, sitting next to him, was as gentle as a sleeping pool. Mrs Wojtys sat ensconced in her plumpness, from which she emerged to preside over the progress of the meal with a kind of self-sacrificing devotion which I had not expected, and every now and then Fuchs said something in a pale, white, phlegmatic voice. I ate a tart, oh, how sleepy I still felt, and there was talk about how dusty it was, and someone said the season hadn't started yet, and I asked whether the nights were cooler here. We finished the pastry, stewed fruit appeared, and when that was finished Katasia came in again and planted on the table next to Lena an ashtray covered with a criss-cross wire mesh which acted as a reminder, a pale reminder, of that other mesh (that of the springs of the bed) on which Lena had been lying when I went into the bedroom and saw her foot and a short length of her calf, etc., etc. Katasia's gliding lip moved quite close to Lena's mouth.

I was hooked. I had fled from Warsaw to get away from things, and here I was, starting all over again, getting mixed up in things here. For a brief moment I was hooked. But Katasia went away again, Lena pushed the ashtray towards the middle of the table, I lit a cigarette, and someone switched on the radio. Mr Wojtys drummed on the table with his finger-tips and hummed a little tune, something like tri-li-li-lee, but stopped, drummed on the table again, started humming again, and then stopped again. The room was too small, it was cramped. Lena kept her mouth either closed or half open, she was very timid and reserved. And that was all. Good night, we're going up to bed.

While we were undressing Fuchs resumed his complaints

about Drozdowski, his chief at the office. He complained in a pale, white voice, standing there with his red hair and holding his shirt in his hand.

'At first we got on splendidly, but then somehow everything went wrong, I started getting on his nerves and I still do, I can't lift my little finger without getting on his nerves. Do you realize what it's like to get on your chief's nerves seven hours a day every day of the week? He can't stand me, he spends seven hours a day obviously trying not to look at me, and if he does by any chance catch sight of me a look comes into his eyes as if he had touched a red-hot poker. And that goes on for seven hours a day.

'I'm at my wit's end,' he went on, staring at his shoes, 'sometimes I feel like going down on bended knee and imploring him to forgive me. But he hasn't got anything to forgive me for. I don't believe he really bears me any ill will, I just get on his nerves and that's all there is to it. My colleagues tell me the only thing to do is to keep as quiet as possible and avoid attracting his attention as much as possible, but'—he looked at me wide-eyed, like a melancholy fish—'what can I do about attracting or not attracting his attention since we are cooped up in the same office for seven hours a day and I only have to cough or move my hand for him to come out in a rash? Do I stink, by any chance?'

These lamentations of the rejected Fuchs linked up in my mind with my own discontented, resentful departure from Warsaw robbed of . . . and in that rented room in a strange house we had hit upon by pure chance the two of us undressed like men rejected and repulsed. We went on talking for a bit about the Wojtyses and the family environment, and I dropped off to sleep. Then I woke up. It was dark. It took me some time to realize where I was, lying in bed between the wardrobe, the table and the water-jug, and I had to make an intense and prolonged intellectual effort to realize my position in relation to the windows and the door. I spent a long time wondering whether to go to sleep again or not. As I had no desire either to go to sleep or to get up, I spent quite a time racking my brains whether to do either or just to stay there lying awake. Eventually I put out one leg and sat up in bed, and as I did so caught sight of the whitish patch of the window. I tiptoed over to it and lifted the blind. Beyond the garden, on the other side of the fence and the road, was the place where the sparrow was hanging in a maze of branches, and underneath it was black earth, and an old cardboard box and a sheet of corrugated iron and other junk were lying about, over there where the tips of the pine-trees were bathed in the light of the starry night. I dropped the blind again and stopped still, for it struck me that Fuchs might have been watching me.

Actually I couldn't hear him breathing. If he wasn't asleep he must have seen me looking out of the window. There would have been nothing out of the way about this but for the sparrow and the night, the sparrow in the night, the combination of the sparrow and the night. If I had looked out of the window it could only have been because of the sparrow, and this made me feel ashamed. But the silence was so complete and protracted that it suddenly dawned on me that he was not in the room; and indeed he was not, his bed was empty. Once more I pulled up the blind, and the gleam from the star-filled sky revealed the place where he ought to have been. Where could he have gone?

To the bathroom? No, the slight sound of water that came from it showed that it was empty. But in that case. . . . Supposing he had gone to see the sparrow? I don't know where I got the idea from, but it struck me that it was by no means impossible, he might very well have gone to have a look at it, he was very interested in it, perhaps he was searching the bushes for an explanation, that reddish, expressionless face of his was well suited to a search of that kind, it was very like him to be racking his brains and working out theories about who could have hanged the sparrow and why. And one of the reasons for his picking on this house might well have been the sparrow (this idea struck me as being rather exaggerated, I kept it in the background, in reserve, so to speak), but at all events he had woken up, or perhaps he had not gone to sleep, curiosity had got the better of him, he had got up and gone out, perhaps to check some detail and have a look round in the middle of the night. Was he playing the detective? I felt inclined to think so. I grew more and more inclined to think so. There was no real objection to this, of course, but I should have preferred our stay with the Wojtyses not to have started with such nocturnal adventures, and another thing was that I was slightly annoyed at the sparrow's coming back and haunting us like this, flaunting itself in front of us as if it were swelling and inflating itself and making itself out to be more important and interesting than it really was. If the fool had really gone to see it, it was becoming a personality who received visitors. I smiled. But what was I to do? I didn't know what to do. As I hadn't the slightest desire to go back to bed, I slipped on my trousers, opened the door and peeped out into the corridor. It was empty and rather chilly. It was a trifle less dark on the left, where the staircase was, there was a small window there. I listened, but there was not a sound to be heard, so I crept out into the corridor, feeling mildly irritated that he should have crept out furtively and that I was now doing the same. . . . The fact of the matter was that two of us behaving like this didn't look very innocent. Outside the room I reconstructed in my mind the plan of the house, the arrangement of the rooms, walls, landings, corridors, furniture, and also its occupants, who were still strangers to me, I had scarcely even begun to get to know them yet.

Here I was in the middle of the night in the corridor of a strange house, wearing only shirt and trousers. This suggested sensuality, a creeping and gliding like that of Katasia's lip, perhaps creeping towards her room. Where was her room? Was she asleep? Asking myself this question promptly turned me into a sensualist in shirt and trousers creeping barefoot down the corridor towards her; and that gliding, darting, reptilian, lip disfigurement, reinforced to some extent by my setback in Warsaw, where my family had coldly and disagreeably rejected me, impelled me coldly in that sleeping house towards her indecency. . . . Where was her room? I advanced a few paces, reached the staircase, and looked out of the window, the only one in the corridor. It was on the other side of the house, the side opposite the road and the sparrow, and I looked out on to a big open space enclosed by a wall and lit by clouds and swarms of stars. Immediately below the small garden was exactly like the one in the front, with gravel paths and meagre young trees, and beyond it the ground was bare, with nothing to see but a pile of bricks and a hut. On the left, right up against the house, there was a kind of outhouse, no doubt that was where the kitchen or the wash-house was, and perhaps it was there too that Katasia was lying asleep, nursing that sinister mouth of hers.

There was an incredible profusion of stars in the moonless sky, and the constellations stood out. I picked out and identified some of them, the Great Bear and the Scales, for instance, but others unknown to me were also glowering and waiting to be identified, as if they were inscribed on the map of the night sky by the positioning of the most important stars, and I tried to work out the lines that made the various shapes. But trying to decipher the map suddenly exhausted me, so I turned my attention to the garden, though here too I was quickly exhausted by the profusion of things, such as the chimney, a pipe, the bends in the gutter, or a young tree, and the moulding on the wall, as well as more difficult because more complicated things such as the bending and disappearance of the path or the rhythm of the shadows. But in spite of myself I started working out shapes and relationships, I felt tired, impatient, and irritated, until I realized that what attracted or perhaps captivated me about these things was one thing's being behind another; the pipe was behind the chimney, for instance, and the wall behind the angle formed by the kitchen . . . just as Katasia's mouth had been behind Lena's when she put the ashtray with the mesh lid on the table and bent over her and put that darting, gliding lip near hers. . . . I was more surprised by this than was right and proper, I rather tended to exaggeration in general, and also the constellations, the Great Bear, etc., superimposed something painfully cerebral upon me. Their mouths together? I said to myself, and a detail that particularly surprised me was that in retrospect and imagination the two women's mouths seemed to be in closer relationship now than they had at dinner. I actually shook my head as if to pull myself together, but the connection between Lena's lips and Katasia's only became the plainer. But then I smiled, because there was really nothing whatever in common between Katasia's dissolute perverseness, that indecent, gliding mouth movement, and Lena's fresh, virginal, half-open lips, except that they were 'related' to each other as on a map, just as one town on a map is related to another—I could not get the idea of maps out of my head, maps of the night sky or ordinary geographical maps showing towns, etc. In reality there was no link whatever between those two mouths, I had merely seen one in relation to the other, it had been an accident of distance, angle and position, and there was no more to it than that. But the fact remained that I, considering that Katasia's mouth must certainly be somewhere in the neighbourhood of the kitchen (where she slept), kept asking myself where, in which direction and at what distance from that spot Lena's little mouth might be; and the cold sensuality that drove me down the corridor towards Katasia was deflected by Lena's accidental intrusion.

A growing distraction was associated with this, and there was nothing surprising about that, for excessive concentration leads to distraction, looking at one thing masks everything else—when we stare at a single point on a map we are quite well aware that the others elude us. With my mind fixed on the garden, the sky, and that pair of mouths, I was perfectly well aware that something was eluding me, something important. . . . Oh, Fuchs, of course. Where on earth was he and what was he doing? Playing the sleuth? If only it didn't lead to trouble. It was depressing to be sharing a room with that fish-like individual whom I hardly knew. In front of me the garden, the little trees, the paths that ended in an open space extending to a surprisingly white wall with a pile of bricks in the middle of it, the whole scene, now struck me as a visible reminder of what I could not see: that is, the other side of the house, where there was also a bit of garden bounded by a fence, and beyond it the road and then that thicket . . . and the tension of the light of the stars fused inside me with that of the hanged sparrow. Was that where Fuchs was, with the sparrow?

The sparrow, the sparrow. The truth of the matter was that I was not really interested either in the sparrow or in Fuchs. What I was much more interested in was that mouth, or so it seemed to me in my distraction. So I dropped the sparrow to concentrate on the mouth, and a kind of exhausting game of tennis set in, for the sparrow returned me to the mouth and the mouth returned me to the sparrow, I was the ball in the middle, and each was hidden by the other. As soon as I caught the mouth, really caught it, as if I had lost it, I was aware that besides this side of the house there was the other, and that besides the mouth there was the lonely, hanged sparrow. And the worst of it was that it was impossible to place the sparrow on the same map as the mouth, it belonged to an entirely different one, a different area altogether, a fortuitous and entirely absurd and irrelevant area, so why did it keep on haunting me, it had no right to. No, it had no right to. No right to? The less excuse there was for it, the more it obsessed me, the more difficult it was to shake off; the less right it had, the closer it clung and the more significant it became.

I stayed in the corridor a little longer, torn between the sparrow and the mouth. Then I went back to the room, got back into bed, and went to sleep more quickly than might have been expected.

Next morning Fuchs and I took out our books and papers and settled down to work. I did not ask him what he had been doing during the night, and I recalled my own nocturnal adventures in the corridor with no pleasure whatever. I felt like someone who knows he has gone too far and consequently feels ill at ease, yes, that was it, I felt ill at ease, but there was an equivocal air about Fuchs too. He set about his calculations in silence. These were very difficult and complicated, covered sheet after sheet of paper, and were embellished with logarithms; his object was to discover a system for winning at roulette, and he was perfectly well aware that this was a crackpot enterprise, a complete and total waste of time, but he devoted all his energy to the task because he had nothing, absolutely nothing, better to do, he was in a hopeless situation, in a fortnight his leave would be over and he would have to go back to the office and to Drozdowski, who would make superhuman efforts to avoid looking in his direction, and there was absolutely no way out of his plight, because even if he outdid himself in conscientiousness and efficiency Drozdowski would find that intolerable too. . . . He yawned and his eyes contracted to two slits, and he no longer even complained. He relapsed into apathy, which was his real state, and at most tried sympathizing with me about my troubles with my family. We've all got our own troubles, haven't we? They've got their knife into you too, to hell with the lot of them.

In the afternoon we took the bus to Krupowki to do some shopping. Dinner-time approached. I waited for it impatiently, because after the previous night's adventures I was very curious to see Lena and Katasia, Katasia with Lena. In the meantime I avoided thinking about them; I wanted to have another look at them first.

But a totally unexpected factor changed the whole set up. Lena was married. Her husband appeared after we had started dinner. I scrutinized her sexual partner with distasteful curiosity while he bent his long nose over his plate. I was utterly taken aback. Not that I felt jealousy for the man, but Lena had changed completely in my eyes, she had been utterly transformed by this stranger who was so completely initiated into all the secrets of her mouth. They had obviously been married only recently, he rested his hand on hers and looked into her eyes. What was he like? He was tall, well-built, inclined to stoutness and very intelligent. By profession he was an architect, and he was now engaged on building a hotel. He did not talk very much and helped himself to a radish. But what was he like? What was he like? And what were they like when they were alone together, what was he like with her and what was she like with him? When a man suddenly comes between you and a woman in whom you are interested there's nothing agreeable about it, but it's worse still if, though a complete stranger, he suddenly becomes the subject of your enforced curiosity and you have to guess his most secret tastes and inclinations and, in spite of your repugnance, you have to divine these through the woman. Attractive in herself as she was, I don't know whether I wanted her to turn out to be repugnant to him or to be even more attractive to the man of her choice. Both alternatives were equally appalling.

Were they in love? Passionately? Rationally? Romantically? Were their relations easy or difficult? Or were they not in love at all? Here, at table, in the presence of the family, they displayed the normal affection of a young couple, but it was impossible to scrutinize them closely, one could do no more than glance casually at them every now and then, resort to borderline manœuvres without infringing the border. I could not very well stare into the man's eyes, so my passionate and pretty revolting conjectures had to be based exclusively on inspection of his hand resting on the table opposite me, near hers. The hand was long and well cared-for, and his fingers and short-cut nails were not displeasing. I examined it, with growing fury at having to try to discover its erotic possibilities as if I had been Lena.

I discovered nothing at all. It appeared to be a perfectly decent hand, but what did appearances signify? Everything depended on the way he touched her, and I could very well imagine his touching her decently, or indecently, or passionately, brutally and furiously, or simply conjugally. But I discovered nothing at all, absolutely nothing whatever, for why should not ordinary, well shaped hands touch each other in abnormal or even disgusting fashion, how could one tell? It was hard to believe that a healthy, decent hand could commit extreme indecencies, but it was sufficient to imagine that it *might*, and that *might* made the indecency the greater. And if I was totally unable to find out anything whatever from their hands, what was I to think about individuals further in the background, where I was afraid even of looking? I knew that if he so much as secretly and surreptitiously linked his little finger with hers it would be sufficient to turn both of them into supremely dissolute personalities, though he, Louis, at that moment was merely remarking that he had brought the photos, that they had come out excellently, and that he would show them to us after dinner.

Fuchs told the story of how we had found the sparrow. 'What an extraordinary thing,' he said in conclusion. 'Can you imagine anybody actually hanging a sparrow? That's really going too far.'

'Yes, it really is,' Leo said politely, only too happy to be able to agree. 'But what sadism.'

'It must have been juvenile delinquents,' his wife Kulka announced sharply and conclusively, removing a thread from his sleeve. Again he was only too pleased to be able to agree.

'Yes, delinquents,' he said approvingly, whereupon Kulka rounded on him and exclaimed:

'Why do you always have to contradict?'

'But I didn't contradict, darling, I agreed completely with what you said.'

'But I said it was delinquents,' she announced as if he had said something different.

'But that's exactly what I said.'

'You don't know what you're talking about.'

She adjusted the handkerchief in his breast-pocket.

Katasia advanced from the sideboard to clear the table, and her deformed, gliding, darting mouth approached the mouth opposite me. This was the moment I had been impatiently awaiting, but I controlled myself and looked away, in order not to interfere or intervene in any way, because I wanted the experience to be completely objective. One mouth 'came into relationship' with the other, and I simultaneously saw Lena's husband saying something to her, Leo intervening in the conversation, Katasia moving busily round the table and one mouth coming into relationship with the other, like one star with another, and this oral constellation confirmed the reality of my nocturnal adventure that I wished to reject. Those two mouths together, the gliding, darting horror of the one in conjunction with the pure, gentle, half closing and half opening of the other. . . . I succumbed to a kind of quivering astonishment at the fact that two mouths that had nothing in common could nevertheless have something in common, it bewildered me, and more particularly it plunged me into a state of incredible distraction—a gloomy distraction impregnated with night and saturated, so to speak, with the events of the day before.

Louis wiped his mouth with his napkin, folded it neatly (he seemed very clean and respectable, but might there not be something pretty dirty about that?) and said in his deep baritone voice that just about a week previously he had himself seen a chicken hanging from a pine-tree at the edge of the road, but he had not taken any particular notice of it, and in any case a few days later it had disappeared.

'But what an extraordinary thing,' Fuchs exclaimed. 'Hanging sparrows, and now hanging chickens. Do you suppose it presages the end of the world? How high was the chicken hanging? How far was it from the road?"

He asked these questions because Drozdowski could not stand him and he hated Drozdowski and did not know what to do about it. He helped himself to a radish.

'Delinquents,' Kulka repeated. Like a good housewife, she rearranged the bread left in the bread-basket and removed some crumbs. 'Juvenile delinquents. Nowadays young people are allowed to do whatever they like.'

'That's true,' Leo agreed.

'But the point,' Fuchs said in his white voice, 'the point is that both the sparrow and the chicken were too high up for it to have been done by anyone but an adult.'

'If it wasn't done by juvenile delinquents, who could it have been?' said Leo. 'Are you suggesting, my dear sir, that it might have been a lunatic? I have not heard of any lunatics in the neighbourhood.'

He hummed tri-li-li-lee again, concentrated on making some little bread-pellets, carefully arranged them in a straight line on the table-cloth, and then contemplated them. Katasia placed the ashtray with the meshwork lid in front of Lena, who dropped the ash from her cigarette in it. The meshwork reminded me of her leg on the springs of the bed, but I was distracted, what with one mouth over another mouth, the hanged sparrow and the hanged chicken, Lena's husband and Lena, the chimney behind the gutter, lips behind lips, mouth behind mouth, shrubs and paths, trees and road. There was too much of it, wave upon wave without rhyme or reason, I was plunged in a bottomless pit of distraction and bewilderment, I was lost and astray. A bottle was standing on a shelf over in the corner, and something, perhaps a bit of cork, was stuck to the neck.

I concentrated on that bit of cork, took refuge with it until it was time to go to bed, I was sleepy and soon dropped off to sleep, and during the next few days nothing happened at all, they were a hotch-potch of words and happenings and meals and going downstairs and coming up again, though I discovered (1) that Lena was a language teacher and had been married to Louis for barely two months, and that they had spent their honeymoon at Hela on the Baltic and were living here until their house was ready (Katasia told me this while conscientiously going about her business, duster in hand); and (2) that (in Kulka's words) 'the scar ought to be reopened and sewn up again, the surgeon, he's an old friend of Leo's, told me so himself, how many times have I told her I would pay for the operation myself, because, even though she's a peasant girl from Grojec, she's a niece of mine, but I don't disown my poor relations, and in any case it's un-aesthetic, it offends the aesthetic sense, it's quite revolting in fact, and how many times have I hold her so during all these years, because do you realize that it's already five years since it happened? It was an accident, you know, a bus ran into a tree, it might have been far worse, how many times have I told her not to put it off any longer but to go and see the surgeon and have it done, because she looks so dreadful, but it's no good, she's afraid of the operation, she always says she's going to do something about it, but she never does, and so it goes on. We've got used to it, and nowadays it's only when someone calls attention to it that we notice it, I'm very sensitive in aesthetic matters of course, but there's all the housework to be done as you can see for yourself, the washing and the cleaning and one thing after another for Leo and Lena and Louis, what with one thing and another I'm busy from morning to night, I never have a free moment, but perhaps when Louis and Lena move into their house, and how lucky it is that Lena has found a good husband, if he made her unhappy I swear to you that I'd kill him, I'd take a kitchen knife and kill him, but thank heaven everything's all right so far, the only thing is they won't do anything for themselves, neither of them, she's just like Leo, she takes after her father, I have to see to everything, the hot water, the coffee, the laundry, darning their socks and mending and sewing on their buttons and the ironing and the shoe-cleaning and the clean handkerchiefs and the bread-cutting, and they won't lift a finger to do anything for themselves, and, what with the cooking and everything, so it goes on from morning to night, and on top of it there are the lodgers, you see what it's like, I don't complain, of course, they take the rooms and pay for them, but there are always things that you have to remember to do for them, and they all have their own little ways and own little wants, and so it goes on from morning to night. . . .'

There were also many other happenings that occupied and absorbed one during the day, and every evening, as inevitable as sunset, there was dinner, at which I sat facing Lena, with Katasia's mouth circulating in the background. Leo manufactured little bread-pellets, carefully arranged them in a straight line, examined them closely and then, after a moment's thought, picked one of them up and transfixed it with a toothpick. Sometimes, after a prolonged period of meditation, he would take a pinch of salt on his knife and sprinkle it on the pellet, scrutinizing it doubtfully through his pince-nez.

'Tri-li-li-lee.' he would hum.

'Pray papass to your papakins a radiculous radicle, my precious bulbul.'

That meant that he wanted Lena to pass the radishes. His jargon was not always easy to understand. 'My honeysuckling, my meadowsweetipie,' he would call Lena, or if he wanted the sugar he would say to Kulka: 'Don't you see that popopkins wants to sweetify the pillikins?'

He was not always able to coin these verbal monstrosities at will, but sometimes started off in crazy fashion and ended up normally, or the other way about. His round, shiny bald pate with face appended underneath, to which in turn his pince-nez was appended, loomed over the table like a balloon. He often had fits of good humour and told us jokes. 'Do you know the one about the bicycle? When an icicle is mounted on a bicycle it results in a tricycle. Ha-ha!' His wife would adjust his tie or remove a speck of dust from his lapel. Then he would grow thoughtful and tie the corner of his napkin into a knot or stick his tooth-pick into the tablecloth, not at random but only at certain definite spots to which he invariably returned after prolonged

meditation with knitted brows. Then he would hum:
'Tri-li-li-lee.'

All this got on my nerves because of Fuchs, because I
knew that it was grist to the Drozdowski mill that haunted
him from morning to night; for in a fortnight he would have
to go back to his office, where Drozdowski would gaze at
the stove with an air of martyrdom when he appeared. 'Even
my jacket's enough to give him the creeps, he just can't
stand me, and there's nothing whatever I can do about it.'
Somehow or other Leo's flow of talk helped him as he sat
there watching him in his pale, yellow, red-headed way, and
that somehow increased my resentment against my parents
and reinforced my revolt against Warsaw and everything
connected with it. There I sat, feeling miserable and hostile,
reluctantly examining Louis's hand, which was no affair of
mine but repelled and fascinated me and whose erotic poten-
tialities obsessed me, and my mind reverted to Kulka, who
was always working, washing, sweeping, mending, darning,
dusting, tidying, ironing, etc., etc. I was in a state of total
distraction, my ears buzzed and my head swam, the bit of
cork on the bottle caught my eye again, and I looked at it,
perhaps to avoid looking at anything else I used it as my life-
line as I floundered in the ocean, though the only sound
that reached me from the latter was too faint and distant and
diffuse to be really audible. Otherwise nothing at all. A few
days filled with a bit of everything.

The heat persisted. The summer was exhausting, and everything just dragged on. Lena's husband, his hands, those
mouths, Fuchs and Leo, it was like tramping along in the
heat, they just dragged on. On the fourth or fifth day my
eyes strayed, not for the first time, to the end of the room.
I was drinking tea and smoking a cigarette, and my eyes
abandoned the cork and fell on a nail on the wall near the
shelf, and from there they wandered to the cupboard,
counted the mouldings on it, and then, sleepy and exhausted,
started examining less accessible places over the wardrobe,
where the wall-paper was frayed, and then reached the
white desert of the ceiling. But a little farther away, near
the window, the tedious whiteness changed into a darker,
wrinkled zone which had been affected by damp, and in-

spection revealed a complicated geography of continents, gulfs, islands, peninsulas, strange concentric circles like moon craters, and other oblique, fugitive lines. In places it looked unhealthy, like a skin disease, here raging wild and unbridled, there adorned haphazardly with curves and arabesques; it contained the menace of finality and vanished into a giddy distance. Also there were a lot of dots that I could not explain. Almost certainly they were not flies, and their origin remained obscure. Totally absorbed as I was by these things and my own internal complications, I gazed at them, persistently and yet without any particular concentration, until I ended by crossing a threshhold, as it were, and finding myself on the other side. I sipped some tea, and Fuchs said:

'What on earth are you gazing at like that?'

It was stifling and, what with that and the tea, I had no desire to speak.

'Do you see that line there, in the corner, behind the island . . . and that kind of triangle near the isthmus?' I said.

'What about it?'

'Nothing.'

'But what about?'

'Oh, nothing at all.'

After a long pause I said:

'What does it remind you of?'

'Do you mean that shape there?' he replied eagerly (I knew why, it took his mind off Drozdowski). 'Just a minute, yes, it's a rake.'

'Yes, perhaps it is a rake.'

Lena intervened, because we had started playing a guessing game, a not very demanding social pastime well-suited to her modest nature.

'It's not a rake, it's an arrow,' she said.

Fuchs vigorously contested this.

'But how can it be an arrow?' he exclaimed.

The next few minutes were occupied with other things. Louis asked his father-in-law if he would like a game of chess, I had a broken finger-nail that annoyed me, a newspaper dropped to the floor, the dogs barked outside the window (they were two quite young dogs which were let out at night, and there was also a cat), Leo said 'one game only,' and Fuchs admitted that perhaps it was an arrow after all.

'It may be an arrow or may not,' I remarked. I picked up the newspaper, Louis rose to his feet, a bus passed, and Kulka said:

'Did you remember to telephone?'

II

As I am telling this story in retrospect, I cannot tell it as
it really happened. Take that arrow, for instance. That evening it was no more important than Leo's game of chess, the
newspaper or my cup of tea; everything happened at the
same level, combined into a kind of concert, like the buzzing of a swarm of bees. But now I know in retrospect that
the most important thing that evening was the arrow, so I
am giving it a prominent place in the story, shaping the
future out of a mass of undifferentiated facts.

But how can one avoid telling a story *ex post facto*? Can
nothing ever be described as it really was, reconstituted in
its anonymous actuality? Will no one ever be able to repro-
duce the incoherence of the living moment at its moment of
birth? Born as we are out of chaos, why can we never establish contact with it? No sooner do we look at it than order,
pattern, shape is born under our eyes. Never mind. Let it
pass. Every morning Katasia brought me my breakfast in
bed, and the first thing I saw when I woke was that disfigurement over my head, that darting, gliding movement superimposed on her honest, rustic, blue-eyed face. Could she
not have stayed in that position for a quarter of a second
less? Did she not spend a fraction of a second too long bending over me? Perhaps she did or perhaps she did not. I
could not be sure, but the possibility penetrated inside me
together with the memory of my nocturnal imaginings
about her. On the other hand, might she not stay leaning
over me like that for perfectly innocent reasons? I had great
difficulty in seeing anything clearly. Only things can be
properly seen; there are far more obstacles in the way of
seeing persons. At all events, that early morning scene in
which I lay in bed with her mouth right over me engraved
itself daily on my mind and stayed with me all day long,
thus keeping alive the obsession with her mouth to which I
clung so tenaciously.

The heat did not help my work or Fuchs's, we were both tired, and he was bored and embittered and he grew pathetic, he was like a howling dog, though he didn't howl, he was only bored. The ceiling. One afternoon we were lying on our beds, the venetian blinds were drawn, the air was buzzing with flies, and I heard his voice.

'Majziewicz might perhaps offer me a job, but I can't give up my present job, it's impossible, what I'm doing now counts as a qualifying period, and I can't afford to waste eighteen months, it's no use even thinking about it, it's out of the question. . . . Look up there at the ceiling.'

'Where? What at?'

'Up there on the ceiling, over there just by the stove.'

'What is it?'

'What do you see there?'

'Nothing at all.'

'If only I could spit in his face, but I can't. And in any case it wouldn't do any good. It's not as if there was any real ill will on his part, I just get on his nerves, his jaw just drops at the mere sight of me. . . . But have another look at the ceiling. Can't you see anything?'

'No. What is there to see?'

'Something like the arrow on the ceiling in the dining-room, but more distinct.'

I did not answer. A minute or two passed.

'The point is that it wasn't there yesterday,' he said.

Silence. Heat. My head weighed heavily on the pillow. I felt weak. He went on again, as if he were fascinated by the sound of his own voice floating in the gravy of the afternoon.

'It wasn't there yesterday. Yesterday afternoon a spider was letting itself down there, I watched it, and if the arrow had been there then I should have seen it. I tell you it wasn't there yesterday. Look at the line that forms the shaft, I tell you it wasn't there; I grant you the rest of it, the tip of the arrow and the other lines are old cracks, I admit, but the main thing, the shaft of the arrow, wasn't there.'

He paused for breath, raised himself, leaned on one elbow, and the dust danced in a ray of sunshine coming in through a crack in the blinds.

'I tell you the shaft wasn't there yesterday.'

I heard him creeping out of bed, and then watched him standing there in his underpants with raised head, staring at the ceiling. His zeal and his staring eyes, which remained fixed on the ceiling, took me aback.

'It's fifty-fifty,' he said. 'How can one be sure? The devil alone knows.'

He went back to bed, but I knew that he was still staring at the ceiling, which bored me.

After a time I heard him get up again and resume his inspection of the ceiling. He would have stopped if he could, but he couldn't.

'Look at the line that forms the shaft of the arrow. I can make out a faint smell, as if it had only just been traced with a larding pin. It stands out from all the rest. If it had been there yesterday I should have noticed it. And it's pointing in exactly the same direction as the one in the dining-room.'

I didn't move.

'If it's an arrow, it's pointing to something.'

'And if it isn't an arrow it isn't pointing to anything,' I replied.

The evening before, while I was again examining Louis's hand with that rather disgusting curiosity of mine, I had glanced at Lena's little hand, which was also resting on the table, and had had the impression that it was quivering, or was slightly contracted. I was not sure, it was fifty-fifty either way. As for Fuchs, I was displeased, and even angry, at the thought that everything he said or did was because of Drozdowski and their mutual loathing. As for myself, but for that row with my parents in Warsaw . . . but one thing fed on another, the result was cumulative. Fuchs started talking again.

He stood in his underpants in the middle of the room and went on talking. He suggested that we should find out whether the arrow was really pointing to something. Finding out one way or another would cost us nothing, after all, and if it turned out to be an illusion at least our minds would be at rest, we should know that no one had traced any arrow on purpose and that the whole thing was nothing but a mare's nest. How else could we make sure whether it was an arrow or not? I listened in silence, wondering how I could refuse to take part in this project on which he insisted only very weakly, but then I was weak too—weakness had in fact permeated everything. I told him to do it himself if he had set his heart on it, but he pointed out that my co-operation was indispensable if the exact direction in which the arrow was pointing was to be fixed, because it would be necessary to follow it outside in the corridor and in the garden, and that required both of us. His final argument was that two heads were better than one, and suddenly I got off my bed and agreed with him, because the prospect of following a definite line, doing something positive for a definite purpose, seemed more refreshing at that moment than a glass of cold water.

We pulled on our trousers.

The room immediately became full of rational and purposeful action. But, as this was undertaken out of boredom, caprice and having nothing better to do, a certain amount of imbecility was concealed behind it. . . . Besides, our task was no easy one.

It was obvious that whatever the arrow was pointing at was not in our room. So the direction in which it was pointing had to be extended as accurately as possible through the wall into the corridor and from there outside into the garden. This involved some pretty complicated manœuvres, which Fuchs would certainly not have been able to carry out without my aid. I went out into the garden with a rake; the object was to lay it on the grass in line with a broom-handle manipulated by my companion standing at the staircase window.

It was nearly five o'clock. The gravel lay hot in the sunshine and the grass had dried up round the young trees, which cast no shadow. Overhead great white clouds drifted in the pitiless blue. The house looked at me through its two rows of windows on the ground floor, and the glass glittered in the sun.

Wasn't there something human about the way in which one of those windows was looking at me? To judge by the quiet, the family were still taking their afternoon nap, but it was by no means impossible that someone—Leo? Kulka?

Katasia?—was watching from behind that window, and that the observer, whoever it might be, might be the person who had slipped into our room, no doubt during the morning, and traced the line that made the arrow. Why? Was somebody trying to make fools of us? Was it a practical joke? Or was the object to communicate a message? Stuff and nonsense, the whole thing was absurd. The sheer absurdity of it was a double-edged weapon; Fuchs and I were using one edge and acting in a fashion that was by no means absurd, so that I, while engaged in these laborious manœuvres, had, unless I were willing to deny my own actions, to count on the possibility that someone might be looking at us from behind those windows that shone in such dazzling and exhausting fashion.

So I took the possibility into account, and Fuch's watching me from the upstairs window helped. I advanced cautiously to avoid rousing suspicion, raked the grass a little, and then, as if exhausted by the heat, dropped the rake, and pushed it imperceptibly in the desired direction with my foot. These precautions made my co-operation with Fuchs closer than I desired, I behaved almost as if I were his slave. Eventually we established the direction of the arrow; the line led to a spot behind the tool shed near the boundary wall, where the property ended in a plot of rough ground, scattered with rubbish and bricks, beyond the garden. We strolled slowly in that direction, taking occasional detours and talking and pausing every now and then as if to look at the flowers or plants, sometimes making expansive gestures and keeping an eye open for any significant features. So we advanced from bed to bed, from bit of stone to bit of wood, with eyes downcast and mind absorbed by the ashen, yellowy, rust-coloured, boring, complicated, sleepy, monotonous, empty but hard earth.

I wiped the sweat from my face. The whole thing was a waste of time.

When we got near the wall we stopped in embarrassment. The last ten paces seemed impossible, they would give us away completely. So far our stroll through the garden under the watchful windows had been easy enough—a few dozen yards of level ground, after all—though we had been in-

hibited by a kind of secret difficulty that made it equivalent
to a steep climb. But now the slope became steeper and
giddier, and the difficulty of the climb accordingly increased,
as if we were approaching the summit. What a height we
had reached. Fuchs squatted on his heels and pretended to
be examining a beetle and advanced to the wall in the same
squatting position, as if he were following it, and I strolled
off in a different direction, taking a circular route so as to
join up with him again; and so eventually we reached the
wall right at the end of the garden in the corner formed
by the hut.

It was hot. Some long grasses swayed in the breeze, a
beetle was making its way along the ground, and there were
some bird droppings on the wall. But the heat was different
here, and so was the smell, it suggested urine, and I had a
sense of remoteness, as if we had been walking for months
and months and were thousands of miles away at the other
end of the world. The smell was of warm, decomposing
vegetable matter, not far away there was a compost heap,
and rain had worn a little channel along the wall. Stalks,
stems, bits of brick and plaster, stones, clumps of earth,
yellowy things. Again the heat changed and became strange
and unfamiliar. . . . But no, there was a link between this
isolated corner living a life of its own and the cool, dark
thicket where the cardboard box and corrugated iron were
and we had found the sparrow, and this seemed to put new
life into our quest.

It was a hard task. Even if something were concealed here
to which the arrow on our bedroom ceiling pointed, what
hope was there of identifying it in this chaos of weeds and
refuse, which in quantity far exceeded anything that could
be done on walls and ceilings? There was an oppressive profusion of possible links and clues. How many sentences can
be composed with the twenty-six letters of the alphabet?
How many meanings could be deduced from these hundreds
of weeds, clumps of earth, and other details? The wall and
the boards of the wooden hut similarly offered innumerable
possibilities. I had had enough. I stood up and looked at the
house and garden. The big, artificial shapes, huge mastodons
of the world of things, re-established a sense of order, in

which I rested. I decided to go back. I was just going to say so to Fuchs, but the expression on his face made me stop short. He was gazing at something.

In the crumbling wall just above our heads there was a sort of niche, consisting of three little hollows each smaller than the last, and in one of them something was hanging—a bit of wood, less than half an inch long. It was hanging by a bit of white thread of about the same length tied to a piece of brick.

That was all. Again we looked carefully all around, but that was all. I turned and looked at the house and its shining windows. A cooler breeze was now blowing, announcing the evening and restoring life to the foliage that had been petrified by the heat. It shook the leaves of the carefully aligned, staked and whitewashed young trees.

We went back to our room. Fuchs flung himself on his bed.

'At any rate it led to something,' he cautiously announced.

'Yes, but what?' I replied slightly less cautiously.

But it was hard to pretend not to know. First the hanging sparrow and then the hanging bit of wood. A strange repetition that gave increased significance to the former (and revealed how greatly we were concerned with it, though we pretended not to think about it). It was difficult to resist the assumption that someone had used the arrow to guide us to the bit of wood and so establish a link with the sparrow. But why? What for? Was it a joke? Was someone pulling our leg? Someone was playing a trick on us, making fools of us, enjoying himself at our expense. I felt uncertain, and so did he, and that made us cautious.

'I bet someone's trying to take us for a ride.'

'Yes, but who?'

'One of them. One of them who was there when I told them about the sparrow and we found the arrow on the dining-room ceiling. Whoever it was drew another arrow here in our bedroom pointing towards the bit of wood. Someone's playing a trick, trying to make fools of us.'

But this theory didn't stand up. Who would want to play such a complicated joke, and what for? How could he have known that we would discover the arrow and take such interest in it? No, the whole thing was pure coincidence. True, you don't see a bit of wood hanging from a string every day, but, after all, it might have been done for a thousand reasons having nothing whatever to do with the sparrow, we exaggerated its significance simply because we had found it at the end of our search and had jumped to a conclusion. But it wasn't a conclusion, it was merely a bit of wood hanging from a string. The whole thing was pure coincidence. But was it? A sort of pattern, a kind of confused message could be divined in the series of events. The hanged sparrow, the hanged chicken, the arrow in the dining-room, the arrow in our bedroom, the bit of wood hanging from a string, all pointed to a hidden meaning, as in a game of charades, when the letters start combining to try to form a word. But what word? It did seem as if an attempt was being made to convey an idea. But what idea?

And from whom did it come? If it was an idea, then there must be someone behind it. But who? Who would want to do such a thing? Suppose it was Fuchs who was playing this trick on me, out of sheer boredom, perhaps? But no, it was impossible. Was he likely to go to so much trouble to play such a stupid joke? That theory simply did not stand up. Was it just a series of coincidences, then? That would, perhaps, have been my final conclusion if there had not been yet another abnormality that I could not help associating with the whole abnormal business, if the anomaly of that bit of wood hanging by a string had not been backed by another that I preferred not to discuss with Fuchs.

'Katasia,' he said.

So he too had noted at least one of the faces of the sphinx. He was sitting on his bed with lowered head, slowly dangling his legs.

'What about her?' I said.

'A person with a facial affliction like that . . . ' he said thoughtfully. Then he added with a wily air: 'One is what one is, after all.'

He liked this idea, for he repeated it with greater emphasis.

'You take it from me. In the last resort one is what one is.'

Indeed it seemed plausible, if only because of the uncanniness of that lip of hers, that she might have had something to do with the sparrow. But what conclusion could be drawn from that? Was one to assume that she had resorted to such subtle plotting? It seemed out of the question. All the same, some sort of link remained, and these links and associations opened in front of me like a dark, yawning, pit—dark but alluring and fascinating, because behind Katasia's lip there was the vision of Lena's half-closed, half-open lips. I actually felt a violent shock, for the bit of wood linked with the sparrow in the thicket was the first definite sign in the real, objective world (however faint and vague it might be) that to some extent confirmed my imaginings about Lena's mouth 'in relation' to Katasia's; it was only an analogy, a slender and fantastic one, but it constituted a 'relationship', provided a basis for reading some sort of order into the chaos. Did Fuchs know anything about this buccal link or association between Lena and Katasia? Had he noticed it too, or did it come purely from myself? Nothing in the world would have persuaded me to mention the subject to him, and my reluctance was not based only on shame. Nothing in the world would have made me expose the matter to that voice and those protruding, fish-like eyes of his that exasperated Drozdowski. I felt weakened, exasperated and oppressed by his being here with that Drozdowski of his and at my being here with my parents, I wanted him neither as a confidant nor as a fellow-sufferer, and this double rejection was the clue to our relationship. But it did me good to hear him mention Katasia. I felt almost pleased that someone else had seen the possibility of there being something in common between her lip, the bit of wood, and the bird.

'Katasia,' he said slowly and reflectively. 'Katasia.'

But after a short period of euphoria the toneless pallor came back into his eyes, Drozdowski reappeared on the horizon, and it was solely to kill time that he produced a series of clumsy arguments.

'It struck me right away that . . . the disfigurement of her mouth seemed to me . . . but . . . on the other hand . . . in either case. What do you think?'

39

III

THE vagueness and triviality of all this forced us to beat
a retreat. We went back to work, but my distraction, so far
from leaving me, increased as evening fell, and the light of
our lamp was obscured for me by the growing darkness of
that spot at the end of the garden. I was haunted by another
possibility. Apart from the arrow we had discovered, there
was no knowing what other signs might be concealed on the
walls or elsewhere. Might there not be a link, for instance,
between the stain over the wash-stand and the peg of the
wardrobe or the scratches on the floor? We might have
spotted one sign, but how many more that we had not
spotted might be concealed in the natural order of things?
Every now and then I raised my eyes from my papers and
stared at the end of the room (taking care that Fuchs, whose
eyes were no doubt wandering too, should not notice what
I was doing). But I was not greatly perturbed; the baffling,
fantastic nature of the whole thing, which kept dissolving
into nothing, could lead only to conclusions equally unsub-
stantial.

However, surrounding reality was now contaminated, so
to speak, by the possibility of innumerable hidden meanings,
and this continually distracted me, though it seemed absurd
that an ordinary bit of wood should be capable of upsetting
me so much. Dinner came as inevitably as sunset, and again
I found myself sitting opposite Lena. Before we went downstairs Fuchs remarked that 'all that isn't worth mentioning,'
and he was perfectly right, of course; discretion was called
for if we were not to be taken for a pair of lunatics or half-
wits. Well, the dinner. Leo, munching radishes, described
how many years before he had learned from his chief at the
bank, Director Krysinski, the art of what he called incongruence or contrariety which, he maintained, every candi-
date for high position must have at his finger-tips.

He imitated the strangled, guttural voice of the late

Director Krysinski. 'Pay close attention to what I'm saying, my dear Leo, because it is absolutely vital to your career. If you have to reprimand a member of your staff, for instance, in the middle of it you must take out your cigarette case and offer him a cigarette. For the sake of the incongruence, you understand. If you have to be hard and disagreeable to a customer, you must smile, if not at him, at any rate at your secretary, otherwise you risk antagonising him too much. On the other hand, if you wish to be obliging or conciliatory to him, every now and then you must say something quite rude or disagreeable, to startle him out of his torpor, otherwise you won't get anywhere with him.'

Leo went on talking, with his napkin tucked under his chin and with finger outstretched. 'Well, gentlemen,' he went on, 'one day the president of the bank arrived on a visit of inspection to the branch of which I was manager at the time. I turned out the guard, of course, and received him ceremoniously and with full honours, but at lunch I tripped and spilled half a carafe of red wine over him. "I see you were trained in the school of Director Krysinski," he said.'

He laughed. He was carefully buttering and salting a radish, after cutting off its tail. When he had finished his handiwork he spent a moment carefully examining it before popping it in his mouth.

'Oh dear, oh dear, oh dear,' he went on, 'I could go on talking about the bank for a whole year on end, but it's difficult to explain, it's difficult to know where to begin, when I think about it I don't know where to begin myself, there were so many hours and days and years, oh dear, oh dear, oh dear, all those months and years and minutes and seconds. I used to squabble like mad with the president's secretary, God Almighty, what a fool that woman was, and she was a tell-tale into the bargain, once she went and told the director I'd spat into the wastepaper basket. "Are you mad?" I told her. But how could I possibly explain how things gradually boiled up to that little episode, it had been boiling up for months and years, and how could I possibly explain the hows and the whys and the whos and the wherefores? How could I possibly remember all the details after all this time? And what's the good of talking about it anyway?'

He relapsed into silent meditation, and then went on in a low voice:

'And which blouse was she wearing that day? I simply can't remember. Which one was it? The one with the embroidery?'

He emerged from his reverie and said cheerfully to his wife:

'Well, Kulka, my chick, my chuck, my mopsy, how are we, then?'

'Your collar's sticking up,' she said, putting down the jampot she had in her hand and straightening his collar.

'Thirty-seven years of married life, young gentlemen, just think of that. The past has gone, gone never to return, but memories, sweet memories remain. Kulka and I, the two of us on the Vistula together, the blue Vistula, and once it rained, oh dear, dear me, how many years ago was that? I bought some sweets, yes, I bought them from the concierge, and the rain came in through the roof, good gracious me, how many years ago was that in the little café? What a café it was, but it's dead and past and gone and can't be stuck together again. Thirty-seven years. Great heavens alive.'

He fell silent, looking pleased with himself, then withdrew into himself again, took some bread and started slowly manufacturing a pellet. He looked at it with wrapt concentration and hummed tri-li-li-lee.

Then he cut himself a slice of bread, removed the crust to make it square, put a lump of butter on it, spread it, patted it with his knife, examined it carefully, sprinkled some salt on it, popped it in his mouth, and ate it, as if solemnly noting the fact that he was eating it. I looked at the arrow on the ceiling, which now looked vague and indistinct. What? That an arrow? How could we possibly have taken it to be an arrow? I also looked at the table and the tablecloth—it must be admitted that the number of things one can look at is very limited—and at Lena's hand which was resting on it, small, relaxed, the colour of white coffee, warm and yet cool and attached by the wrist to the whiteness of her arm (which I imagined rather than saw, for I did not look as far as that). Her hand was still and inactive, but when you looked more closely you discovered some slight tremors, for instance, of the skin at the bottom of her fourth finger, and sometimes her third and fourth fingers touched; sometimes such embryonic movements developed into real ones, as when she touched the tablecloth with her forefinger or passed her nail along the fold. These things seemed so remote from Lena herself that she might have been a great country full of internal movements that it was impossible to apprehend, except statistically, no doubt. One of these movements consisted of a slow closing of the hand and folding of the fingers, a chaste, fugitive movement that I had noticed before. Had it really no relation to me? Who could tell? It was curious that it generally coincided with a lowering of her eyes (which I hardly ever saw), she never raised her eyes when she did it. Her husband's hand, that erotically non-erotic abomination, that remarkable object that was charged with eroticism 'through' her and in connection with her little hand, also rested on the tablecloth near hers, and it looked a very decent, respectable, sort of hand. Of course, the contractions of her hand might be related to his hand, but it was also possible that they might not be completely unrelated to the way I was looking at them through my half-closed eyes, though the chances of this were remote, I had to confess, about a million to one against. But the possibility, minimal though it was, was as explosive as the spark that causes a fire or the puff that rouses the whirlwind. For —who knows?—she *might* hate this man at whom I did not wish to look more closely because I was afraid—I merely looked all round him, he was an unknown quantity, just as she was. Supposing it was true that, while sitting at her husband's side, she was closing her little hand like that partly because I was looking at it? It was perfectly possible, after all, that slight sin might be superimposed on her modesty and innocence, which would make the latter far more perverse. Oh, the explosive power of a slender hypothesis. Dinner was in full swing, Louis had suddenly remembered something and taken out his notebook, Fuchs was boring us to death and was saying to Leo: 'So that's the sort of

43

dragon she was, was she?' Or 'just imagine all those years at the bank,' and Leo, with wrinkled brow, bald head and flashing pince-nez, was describing in detail this, that and the other, and how, when and why, and saying 'just imagine', and 'no, she didn't use the blotting paper' and 'the table was over there', and Fuchs was listening to him only to avoid having to think about Drozdowski. I was thinking that if it was because of me that that little hand was opening and shutting, though I was perfectly well aware that the idea was totally frivolous and absurd . . . when suddenly there was a commotion, an upheaval, a cataclysm. What on earth could be happening? Kulka's plump form leapt from her seat like a jack-in-the-box, dived headlong under the table, disappeared beneath it. Total chaos ensued. What on earth could it be? It was the cat. Kulka withdrew it from under the table with a mouse in its mouth.

After a due amount of verbal seething and boiling, the froth subsided, the agitation melted away, the cataract returned to its ordinary dinner-time bed, the cat was ejected, and the table, the tablecloth, the lamp and the glasses returned to normal. Kulka smoothed out some unevennesses in her napkin, Leo raised his forefinger to announce the imminence of a joke, Fuchs shifted in his chair, the door opened, Katasia came in, and Kulka asked Lena to pass her the salad bowl. Nothingness, eternity, peace. She loves him, she loves him not, I started saying to myself all over again, she's disillusioned with him, she hates him, she's happy, she's unhappy. She might have been all these things, but most probably she was none of them, for the simple reason that that hand of hers was too small, it was hardly a real hand at all. With a hand as small as that what could she amount to? Nothing at all. But how could she be nothing at all if she made such an impact? No, in herself she was nothing at all, but she made a tremendous impact all the same. Gloom, gloom, gloom. Matches, spectacles, snapshots of her, the bread-basket, onions, ginger-bread. Why could I not look at her directly? Why could I look only at her hands, sleeves, arms, neck, the periphery only? Why could I look her in the face only when a special occasion presented itself? How could I discover anything about her in these conditions?

44

But even if I had been able to look at her freely I should not have found out any more. Ha, ha, ha! Laughter, in which I joined, at one of Leo's stories. Kulka cheeped like a chicken, Fuchs had the hiccups, and Leo, with finger outstretched, said: 'I assure you it's true, on my word of honour.' She laughed too, but only to adorn the general laughter with her own laugh, which was why she did everything, only for the sake of adornment, and if I had been able to scrutinize her to my heart's content I should have discovered no more about her, because between her and her husband anything was possible.

'I need some string and a piece of wood.'

What was this? Fuchs was talking to me.

'What for?' I said.

'I forgot to bring my compass, and I've got to draw a circle, I need it for my calculations. I can manage perfectly well with some string and a piece of wood.'

Louis said politely that he thought he had a compass upstairs which he would be very willing to lend him. (The cork and the bottle, the cork on the neck of that bottle over there.) Fuchs thanked him. Oh, I see, he said to himself. You're a sly one, aren't you?

Fuchs's motive was to indicate to the possible practical joker in our midst that he had detected the arrow on our bedroom ceiling and discovered the bit of wood hanging by a string. Just in case someone present was amusing himself by confronting us with mysterious signs, he would realize that we had seen them and were waiting for the next move. It was only an outside chance, but what harm could it do? I looked at the company in the light of the strange possibility that the perpetrator might be among us, and at once the bit of wood and the dead bird in the thicket returned to my mind, the bit of wood hanging in its little niche at the end of the garden. I felt myself to be suspended between these two poles, so to speak, and our sitting together at the table under the lamp here seemed to have a special significance 'in relation to' the bird and the bit of wood; and this was not displeasing to me, for this strange situation opened the way to another that tormented and fascinated me. After all, if I found out about the bird and the bit of wood, one day

I might find out the truth that lay behind those mouths. (But how? Why? How absurd.)

Concentration led to distraction, but I accepted that, it enabled me to be both here and elsewhere, it helped relaxation. I accepted the sight of Katasia's disfigurement moving this way and that, approaching and receding, appearing behind Lena's head and over it, with a kind of stifled grunt, like someone who has swallowed something the wrong way. Again its almost imperceptible perversity became associated in my mind with the normal and charming half opening and half closing of the little mouth opposite me, and this association, which grew stronger or weaker according to circumstances, led to anomalies in my mind such as debauched timidity, shameless modesty, cold heat or sober drunkenness.

'But you don't understand, father.'

'What? What don't I understand?'

'Organization.'

'What sort of organization?'

'Rational organization of society and of the world.'

Leo with his bald pate was launching as assault on Louis across the table.

'What are you trying to organize and how are you going to organize it?'

'I mean scientific organization.'

'Scientific organization?'

Leo's eyes, his pince-nez, his wrinkles, and his bald pate gleamed with commiseration, and his voice dropped to a murmur.

'But my poor young man,' he said confidentially, 'have you gone out of your mind, by any chance? Organization? So you suppose that all you've got to do is stretch out your hand and take the world and reorganize it, just like that?'

He splayed his fingers like the claws of a beast of prey, advanced them across the tablecloth, and then opened his hand and blew on it. 'One puff and it's gone, don't you see?' he said. 'Gone, just like that.' Then he relapsed into contemplation of the salad bowl.

'I can't discuss these things with you, I'm afraid, father,' said Louis.

'Can't discuss them with me? Why not?'

'Because you haven't had the right training.'

'Training? What training?'

'Scientific training.'

'Scientific fiddlesticks,' he said slowly. 'Explain to the immaculate *tabula rasa* of my mind just how you with your scientific training are going to set about organizing the world, what your objectives and methods are going to be, how you are going to tackle the problem, what model you are going to follow, where and how you are going to begin. . . .'

He ran out of steam and sat there gazing in silence. Louis helped himself to some potatoes, and that set Leo off again.

'What do you know about the world?' he exclaimed bitterly. 'I never went to the university, but I have spent years thinking. Thinking. Since leaving the bank I've done nothing but think, my head's bursting with it, and what are you trying . . . what are you trying to . . . what's the good . . . leave me in peace with all that.'

But Louis was eating a lettuce leaf, Leo subsided and calmed down, everything calmed down, Katasia closed the sideboard door, Fuchs asked what the thermometer reading was because it was so hot, Kulka passed some plates to Katasia, somebody said something about the King of Sweden, the conversation shifted to Scandinavia, and from there to T.B. and injections. The table was now much emptier, nothing was on it but tea or coffee cups, the bread-basket, and folded napkins, only Leo had not folded his napkin yet. I sleepily drank tea, nobody moved, the chairs had been pushed back a bit and we had arranged ourselves more comfortably on them, Leo picked up a newspaper, and Kulka sat as still as a statue. She did that every so often, sitting perfectly still, empty and expressionless, only to wake up as suddenly as the plop of a stone falling into the water. Leo had a wart with some hairs on it on his hand. He examined it, took a toothpick, stroked the hairs with it, examined it again, sprinkled some salt on the hairs and went on looking at it. A smile appeared on his face, and he hummed tri-li-li-lee.

Lena's hand appeared on the tablecloth near her cup. A continuous, uninterrupted flow of minuscule events, like the croaking of frogs in a pond, a swarm of flies, a swarm of stars, in which I floated as in a cloud that enclosed and obliterated me and carried me along in its course. The ceiling was full of archipelagos and peninsulas, dots and dampstains, all the way to the white desert over the venetian blind . . . a countless multitude of trivialities perhaps related to those that interested Fuchs and me, with our little lumps of earth, sticks, etc., and perhaps also related in some way to Leo's trivialities. How could one tell? Perhaps I supposed all this only because I was reduced to triviality myself. I felt so trivial.

Katasia put the ashtray in front of Lena.

That mouth, the cold, hideous, darting and gliding movement of that mouth. Stop, don't, take it away, and the ashtray and the springs of the bed and the leg on it. . . . Silence, a black abyss, a turbulent void. And in the midst of the turbulence (Katasia having withdrawn) there suddenly loomed an irresistible, shining constellation of mouths, with two mouths unquestionably related to each other.

I lowered my eyes, and again saw nothing but a little hand on the tablecloth, a double mouth with double lips, innocent and yet corrupt, pure and yet evil and darting, I gazed at it intently, gasping for breath, whereupon the whole place suddenly started swarming with hands, Leo's and Fuchs's and Kulka's and Louis's, a whole multitude of hands were being agitated in the air. What on earth could this be? It was a wasp. A wasp had flown into the room. It flew out again, and the hands subsided. The wave receded and calm returned, leaving my mind full of all those hands, and Leo said to Lena:

'Multiple adventure, pray papass the inflammable phosphorus to your papa.' He wanted the matches.

'Multiple adventure' was one of the many strange things he called his daughter; others were 'dear donkins' or 'dallying darling'; Kulka made some camomile tea, Louis read the newspaper, Fuchs finished his tea, Louis laid the newspaper aside, Leo stared straight ahead of him, and I sat there wondering whether all that agitation of hands had been because of the wasp or because of that hand on the table. Strictly speaking, of course, there was no doubt that it had been because of the wasp. But what guarantee was there that the wasp had not been merely a pretext for a general raising of hands in connivance with Lena's? Ambiguity lay everywhere, and (who could tell) perhaps extended also to Katasia's and Lena's mouths, as well as to the hanged sparrow and the bit of wood. I was wandering on the periphery. Under the light of the dining-room lamp the trees lay dark on the other side of the road. Sleep. The cork on the bottle. The bit of cork stuck to the mouth of the bottle detached itself and advanced towards me. . . .

IV

Next day turned out to be dry, bright, sparkling, but distracted; small, round, chubby, immaculate white clouds kept floating along out of the blue of the sky, and it was impossible to concentrate. I plunged into my work; after the excesses of the previous evening I felt ascetic, severe with myself, hostile to any form of eccentricity. Was I to go and have another look at the bit of wood and see whether there was anything new, particularly after Fuchs's discreet hint at dinner that we had spotted it? I was prevented from doing so by a sense of revulsion against the whole vaguely abnormal business, it was as distasteful as the result of an abortion. So, with my head in my hands, I concentrated on my books—particularly as I felt certain that Fuchs would be going to have a look for me. His interior void was bound to take him there, though he refrained from mentioning the subject which, so far as we were concerned, was exhausted. So I sat there bending over my books while he fussed and fidgeted round the room. But finally off he went. In due course he came back, and as usual Katasia brought up our lunch. But he did not touch on the subject until nearly four o'clock, after his afternoon nap. Then, lying on his bed, he said:

'Come along, there's something I want to show you.'

I did not answer. I wanted to humiliate him, and the best way of doing so was just to ignore him. This worked, he fell silent and dared not insist, but the minutes passed and I started shaving, and eventually I said:

'Is there anything new?"

'Yes and no,' he replied.

When I had finished shaving he said:

'Come along and I'll show you.'

We went out and made our way to the wall, taking precautions as before in relation to the house, which again gazed at us out of all its windows, and we looked at the bit of wood. You could feel the heat coming off the wall, as well as a smell of urine or apples, and just to one side there was a drainage ditch and some yellowed grasses. . . . Remoteness, detachment, life apart in a hot, buzzing silence. The bit of wood was hanging from its string exactly as before.

'Look at that,' Fuchs said, pointing to a pile of rubbish behind the open door of the hut. 'Do you see?'

'No, I don't. I can't see anything.'

'You can't see anything?'

'No.'

There he stood, boring both himself and me.

'Look at that pole,' he said.

'What about it?'

'Did you notice it yesterday?'

'I may have done.'

'Was it exactly like that yesterday? Is it still in the same position?'

He was bored, and had no illusions about it. There he stood, exuding the fatalism of a man irrevocably self-condemned to boredom, and the situation could not have been more insane and futile.

'Try and remember,' he insisted, and I knew he did so only out of boredom, which bored me. A yellow ant advanced along the broken pole. The stalks of a weed growing in a crevice on top of the wall formed a very elegant design against the open sky. No, I did not remember, how could I possibly remember? The pole might be in the same position as the day before or it might not. My attention was caught by a small yellow flower.

Fuchs stood there in front of me and refused to give up. The worst of it was that the futility of our boredom at that isolated spot was superimposed on the futility of those so-called signs which were not signs. The whole thing was too stupid for words. There were two futilities, and we were in between them. I yawned. Fuchs said:

'Look what it's pointing to.'

'What is it pointing to?'

'Katasia's room.'

It was indeed pointing directly to her little bedroom next to the kitchen in the outhouse.

'Good heavens alive.'

'Exactly. If it hasn't been moved since yesterday, it means nothing at all, it's completely immaterial, but if it has been moved, it must have been to guide us towards Katasia. Someone must have taken my hint at dinner that we were on the trail and come here during the night and pointed the pole towards her room. It's like another arrow. He knew we would come back to see whether there was some new sign.'

'But what makes you sure the pole has been moved?'

'I can't be sure, but it rather looks to me as if it has. There's a mark in the sawdust that suggests it was in a different position yesterday. And look at those three stones—and those three pegs, and those three grass stalks that have been pulled out, and those three buttons that must have come from a saddle. Don't you see?'

'What?'

'They form a sort of series of triangles pointing towards the pole, as if someone were trying to draw our attention to it. Don't you see that they form a kind of pattern leading to the pole? Surely that means. . . . But what do you think?'

I tore my eyes away from the yellow ant which was appearing and disappearing among the harness, going now right and now left, now forward and now back. I was hardly listening, I was listening with only one ear, how foolish, pitiful and humiliating was all this excitement about a lot of odds and ends lying under a wall, to say nothing of poor Fuchs's red, rejected face and fish-like eyes. I started arguing. Who on earth would have taken the trouble to leave clues so tenuous as to be practically invisible? How could we have been expected to notice that the pole had been moved? Only a person not quite right in the head could have. . . . He interrupted.

'And what,' he said, 'leads you to suppose that it was someone who was not quite right in the head? And how do you know how many clues he may have left for us? We may have discovered only about one per cent.'

He made a gesture embracing the house and garden.

'The place may be swarming with clues.'

We stood there motionless. I noticed a wrinkled patch of earth, and a cobweb. It was obvious that we were not going to leave things where they stood. What else were we to do but follow the trail? I picked up a piece of broken brick, examined it, put it back again, and said:

'Well, what are we going to do about it? Explore where the pole is pointing to?'

He smiled, embarrassed.

'We've got to. You realize that yourself. To set our minds at rest. Tomorrow's Sunday, it's her day off. We must search her room and see if there's anything there. If there isn't, at least we shall be able to stop bothering our heads about it.'

I stared at the rubbish (and so did he) as if scrutinizing the slight but repulsive disfigurement of a gliding lip, and indeed the rubbish, the swing-bar, the harness, straps and other odds and ends lying about seemed to be vibrating and exuding a sinister atmosphere of perversion . . . also there were the ashtray and the springs of the bed and the half closing and half opening of Lena's mouth and, as she was involved, everything vibrated and boiled and seethed, which frightened me, for, I said to myself, here we are about to act, and by acting we shall create reality . . . and we are going to bring this pole into it, all this rubbish here will bring me nearer to that mouth . . . and I felt pleased, for now, I said to myself, we are going to act, get to the bottom of the mystery, search Katasia's room, solve the enigma, clear it up for good, or banish it to the chimaeras of the night.

In spite of everything I felt better. We walked back along the gravel path like two detectives. Working out all the details of our project would enable me to hold out honourably till next day. Dinner passed off quietly, my field of vision was more than ever restricted to the tablecloth, I had greater and greater difficulty in raising my eyes and looking at the company, I just gazed at the tablecloth and Lena's little hand. Today it was calmer and more relaxed, it hardly trembled at all (though that might point to her having moved the pole). As for the other hands, Leo's, for instance, was asleep, Louis's was erotically non-erotic, and Kulka's was as red as a beetroot. The small red hand at the end of her fat, witch's arm made me more and more uneasy, and my uneasiness was further increased by the sight of the area of her elbow, where redness changed to blue and violet gulfs that gave warning of other concealed zones. Involved, complicated patterns of hands, similar to the involved, complicated patterns on the ceiling, the walls, everywhere. Leo stopped tapping the table, he took one finger of his left hand in two of his right and carefully examined it while a dreamy smile spread over his face. Meanwhile conversation continued at a higher level, higher than that of the hands, though I picked up only a few snatches every now and then. Several different subjects were discussed, and at one point Louis, addressing himself to his father-in-law, asked him to assume that ten soldiers were drawn up in single file. How long did he think it would take to exhaust all the possible permutations and combinations of their marching order, supposing, for instance, that No. 3 took the place of No. 1, and so on and so forth, and assuming that only one change was made a day?

Leo considered the problem.

'About three months?' he suggested.

'No, 10,000 years,' Louis replied. 'It has been calculated.'

'Good gracious me,' said Leo. 'Good gracious me.'

He fell silent, motionless and bristling. The word 'permutations' used by Louis suggested all the permutations and combinations going on in my own mind, in fact I was drowning in them at that moment, and Louis's use of the phrase could be regarded as a strange coincidence—did it not 'almost' amount to an open expression of my uneasiness? How many 'almosts' had I not come across like that? I also had to take into account the circumstance that the reason why this soldier business made such an impact on me was that it seemed to be connected with what was going on in my own mind, and that thus the coincidence was partly (oh, that partly) created by myself, and that that was why I had picked on it instead of on a lot of other things which had been said on which I might equally well have picked. Thus the dreadful, baffling, bewildering thing was that I could never be sure to what extent I was myself the creator of the permutations and combinations taking place all round me. How quickly the thief feels the policeman's eye upon him. When one considers the fantastic quantity of sounds and shapes that impinge upon one at each and every moment of one's life, what is easier than to combine two and two into a pattern where none exists? For a moment the thought surprised me like a wild beast in a dark forest, but then it was swallowed up again in the chaos of seven people talking and eating. Dinner was still going on, and Katasia put the ashtray in front of Lena.

'Clear it all up and get to the bottom of it all.' But I did not believe that an inspection of Katasia's bedroom would throw light on anything whatever. All the same, our plan for next day made the strange relationship between two mouths, two towns, two stars, more tolerable. And was it really so strange, after all, for one mouth to lead to another since everything always led to something else? There was always something behind everything, behind Lena's hand there was Louis's, behind that cup there was a glass, behind that line on the ceiling there was an island, the world was like a moving screen that led you on from one partial revelation to another, it was playing with me as if with a balloon.

Suddenly there was a sharp crack, as if someone had hit something with a stick. It wasn't a loud noise, but it was strange enough to stand out from the other noises. What could it have been? A kind of 'now it's coming' feeling flashed through my head. I froze and held my breath. 'Phantom, show thyself.' But the sound vanished into time, nothing happened, perhaps only a chair had creaked, it had been nothing at all.

Nothing at all. Next day was a Sunday, the day that disturbs the ordinary course of our lives. Katasia woke me as usual, and stayed leaning over me for a moment out of pure good will, but it was Kulka who made the bed and did the room. Moving around with duster in hand, she told me that they had used to have a very attractive ground-floor flat in a comfortable villa at Drohobycz, and that she had used to let rooms there with or without full board, and then they had had a comfortable third-floor flat at Pultusk for six years, where in addition to her lodgers she sometimes had as many as six regular customers for meals, generally more or less elderly gentlemen, each with his own little complaints and fads, one always had to have his special bottle and another his special soup, and another could eat nothing acid, in the end she had had to give it up, it got too much for her, and she told the old gentlemen so, and you should have seen the state of despair they were in, 'My dear good lady,' they had said, 'who will look after us now?' and 'that's just it,' she had replied, 'I put too much of myself into it, do you want me to work myself to death?' Particularly as she had had to look after Leo all her life, and you have no idea what that means, there's always something he needs, I don't know what he'd do without me, I've always given him his breakfast in bed, always, but fortunately that's what I'm like, I can't stand having nothing to do, I'm busy from morning to night, and being busy doesn't mean you have no pleasure in life, every now and then I go and see friends or they come and see me, and do you know, Leo's cousin on his mother's side is married to a Count Koziebrodzki, yes, a Count Koziebrodzki, and when Leo married me his family turned up their noses, and Leo was so afraid of the countess that for two years he didn't introduce me, but I said to him 'Don't be afraid, Leo, I'll stand up to her,' and one day I read in the paper that there was going to be a charity ball and that Countess Koziebrodzka was on the organizing committee, but I didn't say anything about that to Leo, I just told him we were going to a ball, and I spent a whole fortnight secretly getting ready for it—two tailors, a hairdresser, a masseuse and a chiropodist, and Tela lent me some jewellery, and when Leo saw me it took his breath away, but I was as cool as a cucumber, and when we went in the band was playing and I took him by the arm and marched him straight up to the countess. And what do you think happened then? Just imagine it, she turned her back on me. How insulting can one be? 'Leo,' I said, 'your cousin is an arrogant so-and-so,' and spat. But he didn't say a word, that's what he's like, he talks and talks, but when it comes to the point he either does nothing or he's just evasive. But then, when we moved to Kielce and I went in for jam-making, people used to come from miles around and order my jam months in advance.'

She stopped, and went on with her dusting as silently as if she had never opened her mouth. So deep was the silence that Fuchs got embarrassed and asked her what had happened next.

She said that one of her lodgers at Pultusk had had T.B. and had to be given cream three times a day. 'In the end it made you feel quite sick,' she said, and walked straight out of the room.

What did this mean? What lay behind it? And what lay behind that glass I had noticed the evening before on the table near the window in the drawing-room, with two reels of cotton beside it? Why had it caught my eye as I passed? Was there really anything curious about it? Should I go down and have a look and make sure? Fuchs also must have been secretly watching, examining, pondering, for he too was very dispersed, stupidly dispersed, but he did not have even one per cent as much excuse as I had, for Lena was going round inside me like my bloodstream.

I could not help feeling that it was she who was behind all this, that she was aiming it all at me, that she was making shy, surreptitious advances. I could almost imagine her wandering about the house, drawing shapes on the ceiling, altering the position of the pole, hanging up the little bit of wood, arranging things in symbolic patterns, creeping along the walls and in the corners. Lena, Lena, making her way towards me and perhaps imploring my aid. . . . What absolute rubbish! Yes, of course it was absolute rubbish, but on the other hand was it conceivable that there was nothing whatever in common between those two anomalies, the mouths on the one hand and all those strange signs on the other? Could it be a pure figment of the imagination? It was absurd, of course, but could the tension caused in me by the contamination of Lena's mouth by Katasia's be nothing but a chimaera?

Fuchs and I dined alone with Kulka, for Lena had gone out with her husband to see some friends, Leo was out playing bridge, and Katasia, whose day off it was, had disappeared immediately after lunch.

57

Dinner was spiced with an endless flow of talk from Kulka (a phenomenon evidently connected with Leo's absence). The lodgers this and the lodgers that and the lodgers the other, all her life, you have no idea, and what with getting meals and making beds and one thing after another all day long, and one day somebody had to have an enema, and something went wrong with the stove in one of the rooms, can you imagine it. I was hardly listening, but I heard her telling a story about a lodger who evidently tried to take a woman to his room, and there was another who stacked empty bottles behind his bed almost to the day of his death . . . 'I told her not to be silly, she knew quite well where the shawl was. . . . I'm made of flesh and blood, after all, I had worked myself to the bone, I couldn't stand it any longer, and ended by making myself ill. . . . Would you suppose such behaviour possible? Such dirtiness is really too much to put up with. . . .' Her little eyes followed all that we ate, she leant with her bust against the table, the rough skin near her elbow turned a pinky violet just as the patches or warts on the principal gulf on the ceiling turned into a pale, yellowish island. . . . 'But for me they would have died . . . sometimes when he groaned during the night . . . then Leo was transferred and we took. . . .' She was like the ceiling, behind her ear there was a kind of big wart, and there the forest of her hair began, first two or three little ringlets and then the forest proper, thick, greyish-black, twisting and coiling, with wisps here and curls there, and farther on a smooth, sloping area. The skin at the back of the neck was very white and delicate, and there was a mark that looked as if it might have been made by a finger-nail and a kind of reddish patch, and under the shoulder at the edge of the blouse a kind of faded, used-up area began but promptly disappeared under her clothes, continuing underneath that blouse of hers to other indentations and protuberances below. She was like the ceiling. . . . 'When we lived at Drohobycz . . . tonsillitis, then rheumatism and stones in the bladder'. . . . She was like the ceiling, with its zones, islands and archipelagos, elusive, incalculable and inexhaustible. After dinner we waited for her to go to bed, and at about ten o'clock we got to work.

The phenomena ensuing from our activity?

We had no trouble opening the door of Katasia's little room. We knew that she always left the key on the ivy-covered window-sill. Our difficulty was of another kind. We could not be sure that whoever it was who was pulling our leg—assuming that someone was pulling our leg—was not watching us from some secret hiding-place, waiting to pounce on us and denounce our nefarious activities when he caught us red-handed. So we could not be too careful. We spent a long time wandering about trying to find out if anyone was spying on us, but the house, the windows, the garden, lay quietly in the night, which had been invaded by thick, woolly clouds between which a sickle moon darted rapidly. The dogs chased each other in the bushes. We were terrified of making fools of ourselves. Fuchs showed me a small box which he was carrying.

'What's in it?'

'A frog. A live frog. I caught it today.'

'What for?'

'If we're caught we can say it was a practical joke, we were going to put it in her bed.'

His red and white fish-face that Drozdowski couldn't stand. But the frog was a bright idea. I had to admit that its damp slipperiness went well with Katasia's mouth, so much so that it made me feel uneasy, particularly as the frog was not so very far in my mind from the sparrow. Sparrow and frog, frog and sparrow. Didn't something lay behind that? Didn't it mean something?

'Let's go and have a look at the sparrow. It's too early to start yet in any case,' Fuchs said.

Off we went. Among the bushes and the trees there was the same shadow, the same smell. We approached the spot, but our eyes were defeated by the darkness, or rather the innumerable varieties of darkness, that confused everything; there were black, yawning caverns as well as all sorts of other cavities and spheres and different levels all contaminated by a kind of half life, and the whole was plunged into a sort of resistant, inhibiting, viscous fluid. I had a pocket lamp with me, but felt I must not use it. The sparrow could not have been more than six feet away straight in front of our noses, we could see the place but could not make it out, for it was absorbed by the overriding sense of inhibition as well as by the darkness, but finally it emerged, a dark blob no bigger than a pear, hanging from its string.

'There it is.'

In the silent darkness the frog that was with us drew attention to itself. Not that it croaked, but its existence, revealed by that of the sparrow, made itself felt. We were with it and it was with us, communing and fraternising with the sparrow in the avian-batrachian realm, and that reminded me of a darting and gliding lip. The frog-sparrow-Katasia trio impelled me towards the latter and transformed the dark cavern of the bushes into a mouth equipped with that odd, convulsive lateral movement. It was both exciting and repugnant. I stayed there motionless. Fuchs muttered: 'There's nothing new,' and began moving away, and when we got back to the road the night sky was overhead, and the moon suddenly shone out brightly from the midst of a mass of silvery-edged clouds. I felt a crazy need for action, the clean wind of purifying action. I was ready for anything.

The action on which we embarked, alas, could hardly have been more pitiable and pathetic—two petty conspirators with a frog, following the direction in which a pole was pointing. Once more we took in the scene, the house, the slender, white-washed tree-trunks, the deeper shadow of the bigger trees in the background, and the open space of the garden. I groped for the key under the ivy on the window-sill and found it. We inserted it in the lock and lifted the door on its hinges slightly to prevent it from creaking. At this point the frog in the box lost importance and receded into the wings. But as soon as the door was open the cavity of the low little room, from which there emerged a musty, stale smell, combined with that of washing, bread and dried herbs—this cavity belonging to Katasia excited me, her disfigured mouth loomed alluringly before me, and I had to be careful not to let Fuchs notice how hard I was breathing.

He went in with the frog and the pocket lamp while I stayed on guard by the half-open door.

The dim light of the pocket lamp, which Fuchs had

wrapped in a cloth, ran along a bed, a cupboard, a small table, a big basket, and a shelf, revealing in its course new places, things, corners, articles of clothing, dusters and bits of rag, a broken comb, a small mirror, a plate with some coins on it, a bar of soap; a whole succession of things appeared one after the other as if in a film, while the clouds followed each other outside—I, standing in the doorway, was in between the two processions. Though every single thing in the room separately and individually belonged to her, it was only collectively that they created Katasia's presence, a kind of secondary or *ersatz* presence, that I was violating, slowly violating, through Fuchs with his pocket lamp. I was myself laterally displaced standing there on guard at the door. The wandering patch of light sometimes darted about and sometimes rested thoughtfully on something for a moment, only to set off again on its meddlesome, leering, indecent quest for dirt—because that is what we expected and what we were looking for. Dirt, dirt. And the frog was still in its box on the table, where Fuchs had put it.

The dirty comb with teeth missing, the broken pocket mirror, the thin, damp towel, were the wordly possessions of a poor, ingenuous, innocent, decent, domestic servant, partly urbanised but still a peasant at heart, whom we were subjecting to an inquisition in search of some lurking, perverse guilt, of which there was no trace in this mouth-like cavity. We were groping for a corruption, a perversity, a wickedness that must be somewhere here. Fuchs's pocket lamp revealed a big photograph behind the cupboard with Katasia emerging from the frame. Katasia, oh, wonder of wonders, with a perfectly normal mouth, a decent, honest, peasant mouth.

The face was much younger and more rounded, and Katasia was in her Sunday best, a smart, low-necked dress, sitting on a bench under a palm tree behind which you could see one end of a ship, and she was holding the hand of an honest, moustached working man wearing a stiff collar, and there was a pleasant smile on her face.

Sometimes, when we wake suddenly in the night, we could swear that the window was on the right and the door behind our head, but a single clue, a gleam of light from the

window or the ticking of a watch, is sufficient to make everything fall back into its proper place. What now? Reality
imposed itself on us like a flash, everything returned to
normal as on a call to order. Katasia was an honest respectable servant girl who had suffered an injury to her
upper lip in a road accident. And we were a couple of
lunatics.

I looked at Fuchs, feeling utterly abashed. In spite of
everything he was still searching, the pocket lamp was still
nosing about, and it revealed an open account book on the
table, some stockings and some pious pictures, Christ and
the Virgin Mary holding a bunch of flowers. But what was
the point? Why be obstinate? Why not admit our total
defeat?

'Come on,' I muttered. 'Let's get out of here.'

All suggestion of indecency had fled from the things on
which the lamp rested; it was the light that it cast on them
that was indecent now. By our searching and probing we
were sullying only ourselves. In that little room we were like
two lascivious apes. Fuchs looked at me with a mechanical
little smile and went on flashing his torch about at random.
Obviously his mind was a blank, he was as empty as a man
who has lost everything but his shirt and trousers and
nevertheless continues on his way, and his failure with
Drozdowski doubled up on his present failure, and the two
combined into a single failure of unique proportions. With
a smile that had become a brothel smile, the smile of a
voyeur, he inspected Katasia's clothes, her suspenders, her
reel of cotton, her dirty stockings, her knick-knacks, and I,
standing in the shadow, watched him; he was only face-
saving, getting his own back by his own indecency on what
had ceased to be indecent. He went on with his probing,
the patch of light flitted round the comb, and then round
the heel of a shoe, but it was useless, there was nothing, nothing whatever, to be discovered, the whole thing was
utterly pointless and slowly collapsed like a parcel after the
string has been cut. The things on which the torch alighted
were neutral and our sensuality died. The disastrous moment
was rapidly approaching when we should have no idea what
to do next.

But then I noticed something.

It might have been nothing at all, but it might equally well have been something. Most likely it was nothing at all, but. . . .

The light of the torch was resting on a needle. The only strange thing about it was that it was stuck into the middle of the table.

This would have been hardly worthy of notice if I had not previously spotted a slightly more surprising thing, a nib stuck into a lemon-rind. When Fuchs spotted the needle I took his hand and directed the torch to the nib, for the sole purpose of justifying our continued presence here by the semblance of a search.

Then the patch of light darted about in lively fashion again and a few moments later revealed something else: a nail-file stuck into a cardboard box on the chest of drawers. I had not previously noticed it, and the ray of light held it as if asking: What do you say to that?

The nail-file, the nib, and now the needle. The lamp was now like a dog that had picked up a scent, it sprang from object to object, and we discovered two similar phenomena: two safety-pins stuck into a cardboard box. That didn't amount to very much either, but nevertheless in our sad plight it provided a pretext for further action. The lamp got to work again, flitting about and probing. Then we discovered something else, a nail stuck in the wall; the only strange thing about it was that it was stuck into the wall only about an inch or so above the floor. But this was not really strange enough, and illuminating it by the light of the torch really seemed going too far. After that we found nothing at all. We went on looking, but a sort of decomposition set in in the stuffy little hole of a room. Our search petered out, and the lamp stopped flitting about.

Fuchs opened the door, and we began our withdrawal. But just before we left he once more directed the lamp at Katasia's mouth. I was leaning against the window-ledge and felt a hammer under my hand, and I muttered 'a hammer', no doubt associating it with the nail stuck in the wall. But so what? Let's be off. We carefully closed the door behind us and put the key back in its place. 'How windy it is up there,' Fuchs muttered under the vault of scurrying clouds. He was a useless, irritating idiot, and what was I doing with him here? But I had only myself to blame. The house rose in front of us, the pine-trees on the other side of the road did the same, the young trees in the garden were drawn up in ranks—it reminded me of a dance when the music suddenly stops and the couples are left standing, it was stupid.

What was I to do next? Go up to bed? I felt finished, afflicted by a kind of total exhaustion, plunged into a universal debility. I did not even have any feelings left.

Fuchs turned towards me and was just going to say something when the silence was shattered by the sound of violent, sonorous blows.

I froze. The noise was coming from the other side of the house, the road side. It sounded as if somebody were striking something with a big hammer. The blows were heavy, rhythmical, delivered with a maximum of effort and fury— so startling in the silence of the night that they seemed not to belong to this world. Was this aimed at us? We dashed towards the wall as if these hammer-blows, which fitted in with nothing around us, were aimed at us.

On they went. I crept round the corner and had a look, and then seized Fuchs by the sleeve. It was Kulka.

She was in her dressing-gown. Between the long, flapping sleeves she was raising a big hammer or axe and bringing it down on a tree-stump or block of wood. There was a frenzied expression on her face. What was she doing? Was she knocking something in? But what? What was the meaning of this desperate, crazy knocking in of things . . . that we had just left behind in Katasia's room and was now raging here unbridled?

The small hammer that I had touched with my elbow just before leaving Katasia's room had grown enormous, the pins, needles, nibs and nails stuck into things suddenly assumed gigantic proportions. I rejected this idea as absurd almost as soon as it struck me, but at that very moment the sound of other blows came from inside the house, from somewhere upstairs, from the first floor, they were quicker and sharper, providing a corroboratory accompaniment and making my head burst. Panic raged in the night, madness, it was like an earthquake. Wasn't this knocking coming from Lena's room? I tore myself away from Fuchs and rushed into the house and up the stairs. Was it Lena?

But while I was dashing up the stairs the noise abruptly stopped. I stopped on the first floor, panting for breath. The din was over and all was quiet. It actually occurred to me that it would be a good idea for us to calm down and go quietly back to our room. But Lena's door, the third along the corridor, was facing me, and inside me the din was still going on. Hammering, needles, nails, hammering, hammering, hammering, hammering on the door of Lena's room and battering my way in. I started hammering on the door with my fist with all my strength.

Silence.

It struck me like a flash that if the door opened I should start shouting 'Burglar!' at the top of my voice to justify my behaviour. But nothing happened and everything remained quiet, there was nothing to be heard. I hurriedly tiptoed away and went downstairs again. Here all was quiet too, and nobody was around. There was no sign of Fuchs or Kulka. That nothing had happened when I hammered at Lena's door was easy to explain, they must still be out, the noise cannot have been coming from their room. But what had happened to Fuchs? And Kulka? I walked round the house, keeping close to the wall so as to be invisible from the windows, but the madness had disappeared without trace. The trees and the gravel paths lay under the scurrying moon, and that was all. But where was Fuchs? It would not have taken very much to make me sit down and weep.

Then I noticed a light from a room on the first floor, and it was their room, Lena's and Louis's.

So they had been there all the time and had heard my hammering. Why hadn't they opened the door? What was I to do? Once more I was at a total loss, at a dead end. Was I to go back to our room, undress and go to bed? Hide somewhere and watch? Burst into tears? The curtains of their room were not drawn, the light streamed out . . . and . . .

right opposite on the other side of the fence there was a big pine-tree . . . with closely growing branches. If I climbed it I should be able to see inside. This was a rather eccentric idea, but its eccentricity fitted in with what had been going on before. And what else was there for me to do?

The din and confusion of it all made the idea obvious to me, as obvious as the tree that was straight in front of my nose, and there was nothing else there. So I went out on to the road, made my way to the tree, and started shinning up the rough and prickly trunk. Advancing on Lena, making my way to Lena . . . the echo of my hammering on her door was still inside me, and here I was advancing on her again . . . and everything else—Katasia's room, her photograph, the needles and the nails, Kulka's hammering, faded in the face of battering my way through to Lena. Cautiously I climbed higher and higher, from branch to branch.

It wasn't easy, it took a long time, and my curiosity grew frantic. I wanted to see her . . . her with him. . . . What was I going to see? After the din, the hammering, what was I going to see? The trembling that had overcome me outside her door revived again inside me. What was I going to see? At last I could see the ceiling, the upper part of the wall, and the lamp.

And then at last I saw them.

I was staggered.

He was showing her a teapot. Yes, a teapot.

She was sitting on a small chair by the table, with a bath towel round her shoulders like a shawl. He was standing in his waistcoat and shirtsleeves, holding a teapot in his hands and showing it to her, and she was looking at it. She said something, and then he did.

A teapot.

I had been ready for anything, but not for a teapot. Enough is enough, and this was the last straw. There is a sort of excess about reality, and after a certain point it can become intolerable. After so many things that I could no longer enumerate, the nails, the frog, the sparrow, the bit of wood, the pole, the nib, the lemon peel, the cardboard box, etc., the chimney, the cork, the arrow on the ceiling, the gutter, the hand, the hands, etc., etc., the lumps of earth,

66

the bed springs, the ashtray, bits of wire, toothpicks, pebbles, the chicken, warts, gulfs, islands, needles, etc., etc. *ad nauseam*, here was this teapot popping up like a jack-in-the-box without rhyme or reason, extra, gratis, and for nothing, like a fifth wheel on a coach, an ornament of chaos. I had had enough. My throat contracted. This teapot was too much, and I could not swallow it. I had had enough. There was nothing for it but to pack up and go home.

She removed the towel from her shoulders, and I received the shock of her nudity, her breasts and shoulders. She started taking off one of her stockings, her husband spoke again and she answered, she took off the other stocking, and he put his foot on a chair to unlace his shoe. I stayed there, thinking that now I was going to find out what she was like when she was with him in the nude, whether she was vile, sensual, elusive, saint-like, sensitive, pure, faithful, fresh, alluring, or perhaps coquettish. Or perhaps only easy. Or deep. Or perhaps merely resigned and disillusioned, or bored and indifferent, or ardent and full of wiles, or angelic, shy or shameless. At last I was going to find out. Her thighs appeared, first one and then the other, I was going to find out, at last I was going to find out something, at last something definite was going to be revealed to me.

The teapot.

He picked it up from the table, put it on a shelf, and then walked towards the door.

The light went out.

I went on looking though I could not see, I went on gazing blindly into the pitch-black darkness. What were they doing? What were they doing and how were they doing it? Anything whatever might be going on. There was nothing on their part that was inconceivable, the darkness was impenetrable, she might be timid or reluctant or amorous or shameless or perhaps none of these things, indeed abomination and horror might be taking place, but I should never know. I climbed down and dropped gently to the ground, thinking that, though she was a blue-eyed child, she might also be a monster—a childlike, blue-eyed monster. How was one to tell?

I should never know anything about her, never.

67

I brushed myself down and walked slowly back towards the house. Tremendous activity was going on in the sky, great herds were chasing each other across it, black in the middle and shining white at the edges. The moon was hurrying too. It glided, was obscured and extinguished and then emerged immaculate again, the sky was traversed by those two silent, contrary motions. Walking along I wondered whether I should not dismiss the whole thing, shake off the burden, because, as the photograph proved, Katasia's lip defect was due to a purely material cause. So what was the point of it all?

And on top of it there was that teapot.

What was the point of associating Katasia's mouth with Lena's? No, I should not do it again. I should drop the whole thing.

I reached the top step outside the front door. Lena's cat, Dawidek, was sitting on the balustrade. When it saw me it got up and stretched out its back to be stroked. I grabbed it by the throat and started throttling it, wondering why, but it was too late, it happened to me in a flash and I could not help it, I put all my strength into throttling it. Its body hung limp.

Now what was I to do? There I was on the doorstep with a strangled cat in my hands. I had to do something with it, get rid of it, hide it somewhere, but I did not know where. Was I to bury it? Dig a hole in the ground in the middle of the night? Sling it on the road, to make it look as if it had been run over? Dump it in the bushes where the sparrow was? I thought it over, the cat weighed heavily on me, I could not make up my mind, all was quiet. I noticed a young tree tied to a stake by a strong piece of string, it was one of those with whitewashed trunks, I untied the string, made a slip-knot, and looked cautiously all round to make sure I was unobserved (the house had gone to sleep, no one would have believed what a din had been coming from it such a short time before). I remembered that there was a hook on the wall, perhaps for hanging out the laundry. I took the cat there, it was not very far, only about twenty paces, and hung it from the hook. It hung there, like the sparrow and the bit of wood, completing the series. What was I to do now? I was dead-beat, I could hardly stand up, and I was rather afraid of going back to our room, perhaps Fuchs would be there, still awake, and he would ask me questions. But when I quietly opened the door and crept in I saw at once that he was fast asleep. I went to sleep too.

V

KATASIA'S horrified voice, her horrified face right over my head. Just think of it, she was saying, Dawidek has been hanged, hanged from a hook in the garden. Who on earth could have done it? Who on earth could have done such a thing to Lena's cat? This woke me with a start. The cat had been hanged, and I had hanged it. I glanced uneasily at Fuchs's bed, but it was empty. He must already have gone down to see, which would allow me some time to think.

I was as taken aback as if I had not been the strangler. Imagine waking up suddenly and finding yourself in such a situation. Why on earth had I done it? I had had the same feeling of battering my way through to Lena as I had had while hammering on her door. Yes, that was it, strangling her beloved cat had brought me closer to her—though while doing it I had cursed myself for not being able to help it. But why had I hung it from that hook? What idiocy, what blind folly. And to make matters worse, thinking about it while getting dressed and seeing the vague smile on my distorted face in the mirror, I found myself feeling pleasure as well as dismay, pleasure at having brought off a coup. I actually caught myself complacently whispering 'I hanged it'. But what was I to do now? How was I to get out of it? Downstairs they must already be discussing all the possible perpetrators of the deed. Had no one seen me?

It was I who had done it. This shattered me. I had strangled the cat and hung it from a hook, and all I could do was to have breakfast, go downstairs, and pretend to know nothing about it. But why had I done it? There had been such an accumulation of things, so many intertwining threads, Lena, Katasia, the arrows, the hammerings and all the rest of it, the frog or the ashtray would have been enough by themselves, I had been floundering in the chaos, it even occurred to me that the teapot had made me do it, and that I had acted out of sheer excess and superfluity, in other words, that killing the cat had been an extra, one thing too much, just like the teapot. But no, it wasn't true, it had not been connected with the teapot. Then what had it been connected with? I had no time to consider the question further, I had to go downstairs and face the situation which, being still chock-full of the extravagances of the night, was strange enough without that.

So downstairs I went. There was no one around, so they must all be in the garden. Before showing myself on the verandah I looked out of the window from behind the curtain. There was the wall, and the dead cat hanging from the hook, with several people, including Lena, standing round it. Seen from a distance, in perspective like this, there seemed to be something symbolic about the scene. Showing myself on the verandah was no light task, it had all the characteristics of a leap into the dark. If someone had seen me, in a moment or two I should be paralysed with shame, reduced to helpless incoherence. Slowly I walked down the gravel path, the sky was like a vast expanse of white sauce in which the sun was dissolved, it was going to be terribly hot again; what a summer it was. I walked closer, and made out the dead cat more clearly; its tongue was hanging obliquely out of its mouth and its eyes were starting out of their sockets. It would have been better if it had not been a cat, I said to myself, cats are horrible creatures, soft and downy but also liable to howl and scratch and scream, they like being stroked but they also like torturing, they are sweet but they are also monstrous. To gain time, I walked slowly, for I was surprised by the day-time result of my nocturnal deed, which at the time had been hardly visible or distinct from the extravagances of the night. Everybody seemed to be affected by the same slowness, for they were hardly moving. Fuchs was bending forward, scrutinizing the wall and the ground in front of it, which amused me. Lena's sudden and extraordinary beauty took me aback. How beautiful she has got since last night's events, I said to myself in terror.

'Well, what do you make of it?' said Leo, with his hands in his pockets. A wisp of brilliantined hair stood out on his bald head like the pilot of a ship.

I breathed a sigh of relief. No one had seen me. They did not know I had done it.

I spoke to Lena.

'What a nasty shock for you,' I said. 'I'm so sorry.'

I looked at her. She wore a coffee-coloured blouse and a navy blue skirt, and there she stood, withdrawn into herself. Her mouth was soft, and she held her arms close to her sides like a recruit . . . and her feet, nose and ears were too small and too delicate. For a moment this annoyed me. I had savagely and brutally killed her cat, and her little feet were as small as ever.

But my annoyance turned to pleasure, for she herself, if you see what I mean, was too small and delicate in relation to the cat, and she felt ashamed of it for that reason, I could tell. She was too small and delicate for everything, she was just a trifle smaller than she ought to have been, she was useless for anything but love, she was no good for anything else at all, and that was why she felt ashamed of the cat, for she knew that everything connected with her must have an amorous meaning and, though she could not imagine who had killed the cat, she nevertheless felt ashamed of it, for it belonged to her, it was hers.

But it was also mine, because I had strangled it, so it belonged to both of us.

Was I to feel delighted or was I to be sick?

'Do you know anything about this?' Leo asked. 'Did you hear or see anything?'

No, I knew nothing, I had gone out for a walk late last night and when I came back it was well after midnight, I had gone in through the verandah, but could not say whether or not the cat had been hanged at that time. While telling these lies I felt pleasure mounting inside me, pleasure at leading them astray, at being no longer with them but against them, on being on the opposite side to them. As if the cat had put me on the obverse side of the medal and I was now in a realm of hieroglyphics, where occult and mysterious things took place. No, I was no longer with them. The sight of Fuchs, who stopped his laborious search for clues to listen to my lies, made me want to laugh.

It was I who knew the truth, for it was I who had killed the creature.

'Just imagine hanging a cat,' Kulka exclaimed indignantly, and then stopped as if something had happened to her.

Katasia emerged from the kitchen and made her way towards us through the flower beds. Her distorted mouth was approaching the mouth of the cat. As she drew nearer I sensed that she felt she had inside her something related to the cat's mouth, and that gave me a sudden feeling of pleasure, as if it put my cat too on the opposite side. Her lip approached the cat's lip, and dissipated all the doubts her so innocent photograph had put in my mind. She approached with that creepy disfigurement of hers, a strange similarity in lewdness presented itself, and a kind of obscure nocturnal shudder went up my spine. All the time I did not let Lena out of my sight, and oh, my astonishment, my secret emotion, I don't know whether it was pleasure or not, at feeling her shame increase as that distorted mouth approached the cat. Shame is a strange and humbling thing, in fighting off something it draws it down into its own most secret depths, and thus it was that Lena, feeling ashamed of the cat and of the relationship between the lip and the cat, absorbed them into the realm of her most intimate secrets; and thanks to her shame the cat linked up with Katasia's lip like a cog-wheel engaging with another. But my silent cry of triumph was mingled with a groan. By what diabolical miracle could this fresh and innocent beauty absorb such horror and by its shame confirm my imaginings?

Katasia had a box in her hand, the box with the frog.

Good heavens alive, Fuchs must have left it in her room.

'I found this in my room, on the window-ledge,' she announced.

'What is it?' Leo asked.

Katasia removed the lid.

'A frog.'

Leo raised his arms to heaven, but Fuchs intervened with unexpected energy.

'Excuse me,' he said, taking the box from Katasia. 'We'll deal with this later, we'll find the explanation. Now I suggest that we all go to the dining-room. I want to say a few words.

73

Let us leave the cat as it is, I'll come back and have another look at it later.'

Did the idiot want to go on playing the sleuth?

We walked slowly back towards the house, myself, Kulka, who looked disagreeable and upset and said nothing, and Leo, with his crumpled suit and protruding lock of hair. Louis was at his office and would not be back till the evening. Katasia returned to the kitchen.

'Ladies and gentlemen,' Fuchs began in the dining-room. 'Let us be frank. It's obvious that something is up here.'

All this to forget Drozdowski. It was obvious that he had got his teeth into this now and had no intention of letting go.

'Something is up here,' he went on. 'Witold and I noticed it as soon as we arrived, but it was only an impression, there was nothing positive, only a lot of vague signs and hints, so we couldn't mention it to anybody. But now the time has come for frankness.'

'I was just going to . . .' said Leo, but Fuchs did not let him finish his sentence.

'Excuse me,' he said, and went on to recall the discovery of the hanged sparrow on the day of our arrival. Definitely a thought-provoking phenomenon. He went on to describe the discovery of a kind of arrow on the ceiling of our room. It might have been an arrow and might not. It was impossible to exclude the possibility that it had been an illusion, particularly as the evening before, as we would all remember, we had thought we saw an arrow here on the dining-room ceiling. An arrow or perhaps a rake, self-deception was of course always possible. At all events Witold and he, just for the fun of the thing and out of sheer curiosity, had decided to follow the trail.

He described how it had led us to the bit of wood, described the exact location of the crevice in the wall, and shut his eyes . . . we would all agree . . . the hanging sparrow . . . the hanging bit of wood . . . it was just as if . . . there must be something in it . . . if it had not been exactly in the direction in which the arrow was pointing. . . .

I suddenly felt delighted at the idea of the cat's hanging just like the bit of wood and the sparrow and continuing the series. Leo rose to his feet, he wanted to go and see the bit of wood straight away, but Fuchs would not let him.

'Wait a few minutes,' he said. 'First let me tell you the whole story.'

But it was a pitiful story, he got tangled in a cobweb of suppositions and conjectures and analogies, he visibly weakened, at one point he actually laughed at himself and me. Then he grew serious again and, looking as weary as an aged pilgrim, embarked on a long diatribe about the pole and the direction in which it was pointing. 'What reason was there for us not to follow it up?' he said. 'What harm could it do? Having followed up the direction of the arrow, there was no reason why we should not do the same in the case of the pole. Our aim was no more and no less than to establish facts, and what harm could there be in that? Not that we had the slightest suspicion of Katasia, our aim was merely to establish facts. And, to provide against all eventualities, I took with me a frog in a box, so that if we were caught I could say it was a joke. When we left I forgot it, and that's why Katasia found it there.'

'A frog,' Kulka exclaimed.

He described how we had searched Katasia's room, searched and searched and found nothing. But right at the end, just when we were on the point of giving up and leaving, we had noticed something peculiar. True, it was utterly trivial, utterly trivial, he agreed, but when something was repeated more often than it ought to be, well, we knew what it was like when something was repeated more often than it ought to be. But we must decide for ourselves, he would content himself with a mere enumeration. And he began his enumeration, but oh, so weakly and unconvincingly.

A needle stuck into the table.

A nib stuck into some lemon-rind.

A nail file stuck into a cardboard box.

A safety pin stuck into another cardboard box.

A nail knocked into the wall just above floor-level.

Oh, how this recitation weakened and exhausted him. He breathed deeply, rubbed the corners of his protruding eyes, and stopped, like a pilgrim who has lost his faith. Leo put one leg over another, a gesture that implied impatience. This terrified Fuchs, whose self-confidence, in which he was in any case deficient, had been totally destroyed by Drozdowski. I felt furious at being associated with him in front of all these people. As if my own trouble with my family in Warsaw was not enough. What a kettle of fish. But what could I do about it?

'Needles and lemon rind . . .' Leo grunted.

He had no need to say any more to make us feel like a couple of pitiful beggars scratching about on a refuse heap.

'But wait a moment,' said Fuchs. 'The point is that just when we were coming away you, madam, (he addressed himself to Kulka) were knocking something in. With a hammer. On that tree stump near the little door. Hammering it in with all your strength.'

He looked aside and adjusted his tie.

'I was knocking something in?'

'Yes, you, madam.'

'And what of it?'

'But how can you say that, madam? Don't you see the point I am making? Katasia's room is full of things that have been stuck or knocked into other things, and you too were knocking something into something else.'

'I was doing nothing of the sort, I was only hitting the tree stump.'

Kulka extracted these words from a vast, an infinite, store of patience, the patience of a martyr.

'Lena, darling, please tell them why I was hitting the tree stump.'

Her voice had grown stony and impersonal, and the look in her eyes indicated that she was flying the banner of 'I shall see it through to the end.' Lena withdrew into herself; it was less a movement than the semblance of a movement, she was like a snail or certain kinds of plant, anything that withdraws or rolls itself up to protect itself from contact. She swallowed.

'Lena, tell them the truth.'

'Every now and then . . . mother has a sort of crisis. A sort of nervous crisis . . . it happens every now and then. She

76

picks up anything handy . . . to work it off. If it's glass, she smashes it.'

She was lying. No, she was not. It was both truth and falsehood. Truth because it accorded with the facts, falsehood because the significance of what she said—as I already knew—depended not on its truth but on the fact that it came from her, like the look in her eyes or her perfume. What she said was incomplete, compromised by her charm, it was nervous and, so to speak, remained hanging in the air. Who but her mother could understand the embarrassment of this? So she hastened to translate what Lena had said into the more concrete language of an old woman.

'I'm at it all day long from morning to night all the year round, as you know. You know me, and you know that I'm quiet and patient and well behaved. But sometimes my quietness and patience cracks, and I pick up anything handy.'

She thought for a moment, and then said seriously:

'Anything.'

She could not leave it at that, but shrieked:

'Anything.'

'Darling,' said Leo.

'Anything!' she screamed back at him.

'Yes, anything,' Leo repeated, whereupon she shouted:

'No, not anything. Anything!'

Then she quietened down.

I too sat quietly in my chair.

'But that's very understandable, very understandable indeed,' said Fuchs, falling over himself with politeness. 'It's very understandable indeed with all that work and worry. Nerves, of course, that explains everything. But wasn't there another noise immediately afterwards that seemed to be coming from inside the house, from the first floor?'

'That was me,' Lena announced.

'Yes,' said Kulka with infinite patience. 'As soon as she hears it coming over me, she either comes and holds my arm or bangs things too. It helps to calm me down.'

So everything was being cleared up. Lena added some supplementary details. She had just come home with Louis, and when she heard the noise her mother was making she picked up one of her husband's shoes (he was in the bathroom) and started hitting the table with it, and then a suitcase. So that was that. One after the other the baffling riddles of the night were being stranded on the dry sand of explanation. That did not surprise me, I had been expecting it, but it was very sad all the same. The events through which we had been living dropped from our hands and lay at our feet like sweepings—needles, hammers, and all. I looked at the table and saw a jug on a tray, a crescent-shaped crumb brush, Leo's reading spectacles, and a few other indifferent objects, lying there as if they had given up the ghost.

The indifference of these objects was associated with the indifference of these people, which was turning to hostility, as if we were beginning to get on their nerves. But then I remembered the cat, and that strengthened my morale, for in spite of everything a bit of horror remained, with its big open mouth. Also I reflected that, though two noises were now lying helpless on the ground, explained away and impotent, I had a third up my sleeve, a really alarming and embarrassing one that was less easy to explain. What would Lena make of my battering on her door?

I interrogated her on the subject. There had been two series of bangs coming from the first floor, had there not? One had followed the other. 'I'm quite sure of what I'm saying because I was near the front door when the second series began. And it was different from the first.'

Battering my way through to her, as I had tried to do during the night. Had I touched a sensitive spot? What would she say? It was like being outside her door and hammering at it all over again. Did she guess who it was? Why had she said nothing about it yet?

'Another noise? Oh, yes, a little later I started knocking again, with my fist on the shutters. My nerves were on edge. I wasn't sure that mother had quietened down.'

She was lying.

Out of shame, suspecting that it had been me? All right, but what about Louis? He had been with her, he must have heard the hammering, why hadn't he opened the door?

'And your husband? Wasn't he with you?'

'No, he was in the bathroom.'

78

So she had been alone when I started knocking, and she had not opened the door. Perhaps she had guessed that it was I or perhaps she had not, but in any case she knew that the knocking had been meant for her. She had not opened the door because she had been afraid to. And now she was lying, pretending she had done it herself. Oh, triumph, my lie had broken through to hers and we were united in a common lie, and by my lie I had implanted myself in hers.

However, Leo returned to the point.

'But who hanged the cat?' he said.

He pointed out politely that, the noises having been completely explained, there was no point in discussing them further, and in any case he could contribute nothing to the subject as his bridge party had lasted until three a.m. But who had hanged the cat, and why? His insistence was not directed at anyone in particular, but it was ominous and threatening. There was a stubborn expression of his face under the crown of his bald patch. In all good faith and with good reason he wanted to know who had killed the cat. His persistence began to worry me. Kulka quietly interrupted him.

'Leo,' she said.

Supposing she had done it? Supposing she had done it? Of course I was very well aware that I had done it myself, but by saying 'Leo' like that she attracted everyone's attention to herself and Leo's persistence seemed to have attained its object and alighted on her. I had the feeling that in spite of everything she *could* have done it, that if she was capable of battering a tree stump with a hammer in a nervous crisis she was equally capable of a murderous onslaught on a cat. With those short limbs and thick wrists and ankles of hers and that short, thickset body, rich in maternal bounties, she would have been perfectly capable of throttling the cat and then hanging it. It would have been just like her.

'Tri-li-li-lee!'

There was concealed satisfaction in the tune that Leo started humming, but he quickly broke it off. There was something malicious about it.

Had he been pleased that his Kulka had not been able to stand up to the question, that his insistence had struck home, and that she had therefore attracted general attention to herself? So . . . the culprit might have been Leo himself. Of course, why not, he would have been perfectly capable of it. . . . With those bread pellets he made and enjoyed himself so much with, transfixing them with a toothpick, moving them about and arranging them, and the way he hummed and cut apple peelings with his finger nail and spent his time 'thinking' and scheming, why should he be incapable of throttling a cat and hanging it? Of course it was I who had done it, but he *could* have done it. He was perfectly capable of it, just as he was perfectly capable now of taking malicious pleasure in seeing his wife under suspicion. Though he had actually not done it (since I had done it myself), he might very well have hanged the sparrow and the bit of wood.

The mystery of the latter had not been in any way diminished by my killing the cat. They were still hanging as before, like two centres of darkness.

Darkness. I needed it myself, to prolong the night during which I had battered at Lena's door. And Leo perhaps inserted himself into this darkness of mine, for his behaviour hinted at the possibility of licentious sybaritism, secret orgies, haunting the confines of this respectable home—a hypothesis that would not have been so plausible but for the way he quickly cut short his little tune for fear of giving himself away. That tri-li-li-lee of his had been like a whoop of pleasure at his wife's downfall. . . . Was it dawning on Fuchs too that this respectable retired bank manager, this sterling husband and father who never went out except for a game of bridge, was capable of enjoying private pleasures of his own under his wife's eye at the family dining table? If he enjoyed himself playing with bread pellets, why should he not also enjoy himself tracing arrows on the ceiling? To say nothing of other secret vices. He was a thinker, he thought and thought, and he was capable of thinking up a lot of things.

There was a noise, a clatter, a terrible din outside, the whole place shook, it was a passing lorry, a big one with a trailer, the noise faded away again, vanished, the windows stopped rattling and we looked away from them again, but the incident was sufficient to recall the outside world, the world beyond our little group, and I heard the barking of the dogs in the next-door garden, noticed the jug of water on the little table, nothing of the slightest consequence, of course, but this intrusion of the outside world somehow changed the situation and the talk became more disorderly. Somebody said it could not have been a stranger because the dogs would have gone for him, and somebody else remembered that last year there had been thieves in the neighbourhood, and so on and so forth, and so it went on for a long time, but I kept on picking out distant sounds, as if someone were tapping or hitting something somewhere, and a sort of coppery echo like that of a samovar. The dogs barked again, I felt tired and depressed, and then I had the feeling that something was coming up again.

'Who did this to you, darling? Who can it have been?'

It was Kulka with her arms round Lena, they were locked in a firm embrace. This struck me as unpleasant, as if it were aimed at me, and put me on the alert again. But what really put me on my guard was the prolongation of the embrace for a fraction of a second longer than was strictly necessary (which made it excessive and exaggerated).

'Who can have done this to you?' said Kulka, releasing Lena from between her two short arms. 'Who can have done this to you?'

What was she after? Was she aiming at anyone? She was not aiming at Leo, so perhaps she was aiming at me. Yes, at Fuchs and at me. By hugging Lena she was dragging into the light of day all the dark passion that underlay that cat morning. When she said 'who did this to you?' what she meant was 'these two young men who arrived here recently are the obvious suspects.' The implication that the cat was an object of passion gave me pleasure, but danger loomed, I must be on my guard. What was I to say? I hesitated, I was at a loss, my mind was blank, I was at a dead end, at the bottom of a deep, dark pit, but at last I heard Fuchs's voice.

He spoke quite calmly, as if he were thinking aloud, as if what he was saying had no connection with Kulka.

'First the chicken was hanged, then the sparrow, and then the bit of wood,' he said. 'It's always the same act of hanging, though the object changes. And it has been going on for some time, the sparrow stank pretty badly when we found it on the day we arrived.'

Good for Fuchs, he was not such a fool after all. It was a good point, the hangings had begun well before our arrival, so we were beyond suspicion. But what a pity.

'That's perfectly true,' said Leo, and I realized that he too must have suspected us for a time. Conversation sprang to life again. 'Katasia?' said Kulka. 'How could it possibly have been Katasia? What an idea! She's going round like a soul in torment, she's beside herself with grief, she was terribly fond of the cat, she was devoted to it, and I've known her from childhood, and but for all I've done for her. . . .' She went on talking, but she talked much too much and exaggerated as landladies do, and I wondered if she wasn't overdoing it. But I heard the sound of water running from a tap, and what might have been a car starting up.

'Someone must have crept in,' Leo said. 'But to hang a cat? Who on earth would creep in to hang a cat? Who on earth would creep in to hang a cat? And the dogs next door wouldn't have let him.'

My arm ached. I looked out of the window. The young trees, the pines, the sky, the heat. The moulding of the window-frame was made of a different kind of wood. A leaf was sticking to one of the panes. Leo announced that he was going to have a look at the bit of wood and the other clues.

'But perhaps you can see some from here,' said Fuchs. 'I beg your pardon?'

'How can we be sure that there are not other clues in this room that we haven't spotted yet?'

I turned to Lena and said:

'And do you suspect anyone?' She withdrew into her shell. 'I don't think anyone wishes me ill,' she replied.

(This made me realize that I did not wish her ill myself. Oh, to stop living, to die, not to have to go on with it all. What a burden. Death would have been welcome at that moment.)

Leo launched into a pathetic lament.

'How disagreeable, how distasteful, all this is,' he said. 'If only we knew where to begin, but we don't know even that. We haven't got a single hard fact to work on. Whoever it was cannot have come in over the fence, and it cannot have been someone from inside the house either. So who can it have been? It cannot have been either the one or the other, so who can it have been? I feel like sending for the police, but what would be the good of that, the only result would be to set tongues wagging, we should make ourselves a laughing-stock. So we can't even send for the police. But, gentlemen, the point is this, it's not just the matter of the cat. Cat or no cat, there's something strange and abnormal at work, there's a kind of aberration or something in the air, it opens a field for speculation, unlimited speculation, and we are entitled to trust no one and suspect everyone, for who could take an oath that it was not one of us who are quietly sitting here? It's a case of madness, perversion, aberration, the sort of thing that could happen to anyone, me, my wife, Katasia, you gentlemen, my daughter, for if it's an aberration there's no telling, *aberratio fiat ubi vult*, ha, ha, ha, as the saying is, it can happen to anyone anywhere and take any form. But all the same, what a mean and disgusting thing. To think that in my old age, in my own home and in the bosom of my family, I am not able even to be sure of the ground under my feet or in what sort of company I am. To think that I am reduced to being like a lost dog in my own home. To think that I can't trust anyone, that my house has become a lunatic asylum. And to think that all the work and worry of a lifetime, the millions of things I can't count or remember any more, all those years and months and weeks and days and minutes and seconds, that vast inconceivable number of hours, that whole great mountain of hours, each marked by work and worry . . . to think that it should all end in my no longer being able to trust anyone. And I should like to know why. I admit, of course, that it could be said that I am dramatising the whole thing and that a cat is not very important but, gentlemen, it's very disagreeable, very disagreeable indeed, for how can we be sure that the cat is the end of the story and that next time it won't be bigger game? If there's a lunatic in the house, how can we be sure what will happen next? Now, the last thing I want to do is to exaggerate, but how can one's mind be at rest until it has been cleared up? At the mercy of . . . at the mercy of . . . in one's own home at the mercy of. . . .'

'Leo, stop it.'

He looked at Kulka, sadly.

'Stop it,' he said. 'All right, I'll stop it. But I shan't stop thinking. No, I shan't stop thinking.'

'If only you would,' Lena whispered under her breath, and I thought I detected something new in her in the way she did this, something that had not been there before. But how could one tell? How could one tell? I wondered. A car full of people rumbled past, I only caught sight of their heads behind the last bush, the dogs barked, a shutter creaked on the first floor, a child whimpered, there was a general, collective, orchestrated noise from the depths, and on the sideboard there was a bottle and a cork. Would she be capable of killing a child? With that gentle expression of hers? If she did such a thing, it would promptly merge into and harmonize with that expression of hers, and it would be demonstrated that a child murderer could have a gentle expression. How could one tell? The cork and the bottle.

'What's the matter with you?' Leo said irritably. Then he turned to Fuchs and said to him humbly:

'Perhaps you will be able to give us some advice. Let us go and have a look at the arrow and the bit of wood.'

It was hot, the little rooms on the ground floor were stifling at that time of day, you could see the dust in the air, I felt tired and my feet ached, all the doors and windows were open, things kept happening, a bird flew past, there was a universal buzzing and humming, and I heard Fuchs saying: '. . . there I entirely agree with you. At any rate it has been useful to speak out frankly. If anyone sees anything new, he must let us know at once. . . .' Drozdowski, Drozdowski. Everything was struggling slowly out of a glue-pot. It was like someone who has got half his body out of a bog and has struggled to his knees but is going to slide back again at any moment. There were so many details to take into account. . . . I remembered that I had not had breakfast yet. My head ached. I wanted to light a cigarette, and rummaged in my pockets for my matches, but I had forgotten them. There were some at the other end of the table next to Leo. Should I ask him for them or not? I ended by showing him my cigarette, he nodded, stretched out his hand and pushed the box towards me, and I stretched out my hand and took it.

VI

THE CAT was buried on the other side of the fence, in the ditch by the roadside. The job was done by Louis after he came back from his office and had been told everything. He looked disgusted, muttered 'barbarism', put his arms round Lena, hugged her, and went off and buried the creature. It was impossible to settle down to work, of course, so I wandered about. I walked a little way down the road but came back and paced up and down the garden. From a distance, and cautiously, so that nobody should notice, I inspected the pine-tree I had climbed, the tree stump that Kulka had battered, the door of Katasia's room, and the place behind the corner of the house where I had been standing when I heard the knocking coming from the first floor. Hidden somewhere in all these places and things, in the totality of these places and things, lay the path that had led me to strangle the cat. If I could discover the thread running through all these things, I might perhaps find out what had made me do it.

I even found an excuse to go to the kitchen and have another look at Katasia's mouth. But the labyrinth was growing, there was such a proliferation, such a multitude of things and places and events. Is not every pulsation of our lives made up of thousands of millions of tiny fragments? So what can one do? I had absolutely nothing to do. I was unemployed.

I even went to the empty room where I had first seen Lena and her foot on the springs of the bed. On the way back I stopped in the corridor to recall the way a floor-board had creaked during that first night when I went to look for Fuchs. I looked at the arrow on the ceiling, the ashtray, the bit of cork on the neck of the bottle, but idly, with no thoughts in my head, I just looked, feeling weak among all those insignificant trifles, rather like an invalid after a severe illness whose world has shrunk to a beetle or a patch of sun-

light; and at the same time I felt like someone trying to re-
create his own strange and inexplicable past life (this reminded me of Leo, with his myriads of hours and minutes
and seconds, and made me smile).

What was I looking for? What was I looking for? A basic
theme, a *Leitmotiv*, an axis, something of which I could take
firm hold and use as a basis for reconstructing my personality
here? But distraction, not only my own personal, inner distraction, but also that coming from without, from the chaos,
profusion and excess of things, preventing me from concentrating. One trifle distracted me from another, everything was equally important and unimportant, I kept
approaching things and stepping back again.

The cat. Why had I killed that cat of hers? Gazing at
some clumps of earth in the garden, some of those that
Fuchs and I had examined while following the direction of
the arrow (which I had established with the aid of the broom-
handle), I decided that the question would have been easier
to answer if my feelings towards her had been less obscure.
What were they? I kept asking myself, trampling the grass
as I had done on that other occasion. What were they?
Love? But what sort of love? Passion? But what sort of
passion? How had it come about without my knowing what
she was like, what sort of person she was? I still did not
know. Looking at the continents, the archipelagos and the
nebulae on the bedroom ceiling, I told myself she was obscure, illegible, undecipherable and tantalizing, I could
imagine her so many different ways in so many different
situations depending on which way I looked at her, I kept
losing her and finding her again, turning her this way and
that. But (I went on, continuing to spin my thread as I
looked carefully at the ground between the house and the
kitchen and inspected the young trees tied firmly to their
stakes) there could be no denying that I had been sucked
into and swallowed up by the vacuum that she was, that it
was she and she only. . . . And (I said to myself, gazing at
the pattern formed by the bent gutter, the broken one) what
did I want of her? Did I want to caress her? Torment her?
Humiliate her? Worship her? Did I want to be an angel
with her or a brute? Did I want to assault her or take her in

my arms? Did I know what I wanted? That was the agony, I did not. I could have raised her chin and gazed into her eyes, or I could have spat in her mouth, I did not know what I wanted. But she weighed on my conscience, she emerged as out of a dream, heavy with a despair that followed her as her long hair would if she let it down. And that made the cat more horrible than ever.

In the course of my wanderings I strolled in the direction of the sparrow, I was plagued by the disproportionate role it played in my mind. It remained perpetually on the sidelines and kept on obtruding itself, though it was impossible to connect it with anything. All the same (I said to myself, sauntering down the baking road and trampling on the dried up grass), it could not be denied that there were certain analogies, even if it was only that there was a certain relationship between cats and sparrows, cats ate sparrows, after all. Why was there no escape from the cobweb of relationships?

But all that was secondary. What mattered was that something was advancing steadily into the foreground, assuming greater and greater importance and more insistently obtruding itself. It derived from the fact of the cat that I had not just strangled but hanged.

I had of course hanged it for lack of anything else to do with it. After our multiple adventures with the sparrow and the bit of wood the idea of hanging it had come mechanically. I had acted out of rage and fury at having let myself be drawn into a stupid adventure; in other words, I had wanted to get my own back. I had wanted to play a trick on them, so that I could have a good laugh, and I had also wanted to divert suspicion elsewhere. Yes, yes, but the fact remained that I had done it and, though the deed was my own, it associated itself with the hanging of the sparrow and the bit of wood. Now, three hangings were different from two, they amounted to something. The fact of hanging began swelling and growing, assuming tremendous proportions in the torrid, cloudless heat, with the result that there was nothing eccentric about my plunging into the thicket to go and see the sparrow. As I wandered about waiting for something finally to prevail inside me, the necessity of going and having a look at it imposed itself on me by itself. Going and having a look at it? Just before plunging into the thicket I stopped dead, with one foot in the air. No, better not, I said to myself, if you do, hanging will impose itself still more powerfully on you, you had better be careful. If we had not chanced on the sparrow, perhaps . . . or rather it's practically certain. Better be careful. I stayed where I was, knowing perfectly well that the only result of this hesitation would be to magnify the importance of my advance into the thicket, which duly followed. In the shade I felt better. A butterfly suddenly appeared and flew away. I reached the spot, foliage formed a vault of deeper shadow, and there it was, hanging from a wire.

It was still hanging, just as it had been when Fuchs and I found it. I examined the little dried-up ball, which was becoming less and less like a sparrow every day. Strange, I wanted to laugh, but better not. But I didn't really know what I wanted to do, because after all I had not come here only to look at it. I could not think what the right thing to do was, perhaps I ought to greet it with an appropriate gesture, or say something, but no, better not, that would be exaggerating, going too far. . . . How dappled with sunshine the black earth was. And look at that worm there. The round trunk of a pine-tree. If I came here bringing my hanging of the cat with me, it's certainly no trivial matter, but something I have done to myself. Amen, amen, amen. The edges of the leaves were curling, that was the effect of the heat. Who had dropped that old tin here, and what was inside it? Oh, ants, of course, I hadn't noticed them. Oh, that's enough, let's be off. What a good thing you've associated your hanging of the cat with the hanging of the sparrow, that has made something quite different of it. Why different? Don't ask. Let's be off. What's that bit of paper over there?

A few moments later I was opening the little garden gate, scorched by the sun shining in the tremulous sky. Dinner was exactly the same as usual, complete with Leo's usual little jokes and play with words, but all the same the artificiality and feline tension were catching and, though everyone tried to behave with complete naturalness, there was an element of theatricality about their naturalness. Not that anyone suspected anyone else, good gracious no, but everyone was tangled in a net of clues that led nowhere and questions to which there were no answers. Bafflement hung almost tangibly in the air. True, no one suspected anyone else, but no one could be certain that others did not suspect him, so everyone behaved with slightly exaggerated charm and courtesy and felt slightly ashamed of not being completely himself however hard he tried, and of having to make an effort to be what ought to be the easiest thing in the world. The whole of everyone's behaviour being thus to some extent distorted, everything started being related to the cat and all the revelations associated with the creature. Kulka, for instance, complained that Leo or Lena, or perhaps both, had forgotten to remind her of something, and that somehow made her cat-like, as if it were all because of the cat; there was the same element of morbid distortion in Leo's conversation, which kept casting side-long glances in the same direction. . . . I was already familiar with these symptoms, they were on my trail, my eyes grew busy, avoiding the eyes of others, began rummaging in the corners, plunging into the depths, searching and examining the shelf and behind the cupboard; and the so familiar carpet or curtain turned into a desert or achieved the giddy distances of the archipelagos and continents on the ceiling. And supposing. . . . And of course they did not keep off the subject of the cat altogether. No, here they were actually talking about it, because not talking about it would have been worse.

Lena's hand. There it was on the table-cloth, as usual, next to her fork, in the light of the lamp. I looked at it as I had previously looked at the sparrow, it was resting on the table just as the sparrow had been hanging in the thicket. The sparrow was there, and the hand was here. It approached the fork, picked it up—no, the fingers merely rested on it. My fingers approached my fork and did the same. I was plunged into silent ecstasy by this understanding between us, though it was a phoney, one-sided one, existing in myself alone. Next to my hand, almost touching it, there was a spoon, and there was an exactly similar spoon next to hers. Should I rest the edge of my hand on the spoon? The distance was so slight that nobody would notice. My hand moved, touched the spoon, and her hand moved too and touched her spoon.

This happened during a period of time that sounded like a gong and was filled over the brim with cascades, whirlwinds, swarms of locusts, clouds, the Milky Way, dust and noise, events and one thing and another. Had it been a coincidence or not? How could one tell? It might and it might not, her hand had moved, perhaps deliberately, perhaps half deliberately, or perhaps not deliberately at all. There was no knowing. Kulka removed some plates and Fuchs tugged at his sleeve.

Early next morning we went off on an excursion into the mountains.

This was an old idea of Leo's, he had been boring us with it for a long time. He had promised us a treat in a thousand, a really outstanding experience in our own, familiar mountains. Famous beauty-spots such as Tornie and Koscieliska and Morskie Oke had nothing to offer in comparison, nothing but stale picture postcard stuff, commonplace, second-rate tourist attractions, while the mountain panorama that he proposed to lay before us was a song of songs, a marvel of marvels, an unforgettable, an ecstatic experience we would dream about for the rest of our lives. Did we want to know how he had discovered it? He had lost his way and had hit on it completely by chance. How many years ago? Twenty-seven, it would be twenty-seven in July, he remembered it as if it were yesterday, he had been in the Koscielisko valley and had lost his way and had wandered and wandered, and there, three miles off the road, he had come across a panorama that . . . one could go there by carriage, there was even a mountain refuge there, though an abandoned one, he had found out that it had been bought by the bank, who were going to develop it. It was really a sight to be seen, a garland of natural beauty, a dark green dream world of grass and trees and flowers and streams with a poetical whisper everywhere, set in a superb amphitheatre of mountains, it was magnificent, it was breath-taking, it was unique, the mere thought of it was enough to make you smack your lips and lick your fingers, and we could make a one-day or two-day excursion of it by carriage, taking provisions and bedding, we could take his word for it, to anyone who had once been there it was an experience he would remember for the rest of his life. He had been living on it ever since and had sworn to go back. The years were passing, but he would keep his oath.

After the cat incident the prospect of distraction and getting some fresh air into our lungs was the more tempting as we were all stifling in the house. Kulka, after repeatedly saying what absurd ideas Leo had and telling him to be quiet, ended by falling in with the project, particularly after he pointed out that it would be an excellent opportunity of returning the hospitality of two friends of Lena's who were staying at Zakopane. Thus Leo's insistence yielded to intense culinary and other activity on Kulka's part directed to ensuring the success of a social event.

The consequence was that, though the cat-mouth-hand-bit of wood, etc., constellation still survived with all its off-shoots, ramifications and tentacles, a new and healthier trend set in, and we all fell in with the idea. In a fit of benevolence Kulka informed Fuchs and me that it would be an exceptionally delightful occasion, as both Lena's friends had only just got married, so there would be three honeymoon couples, so to speak, which would make it a far more interesting social event than ordinary outings to 'commonplace' spots. This too, of course, was related to the cat. The cat was the moving spirit behind the whole thing, for without it none of us would have agreed to Leo's project so readily. But it also served to distract us from the cat, and so it was a relief. However, the last few days beforehand were imbued with a kind of immobility, as if nothing wanted to happen. One evening meal was exactly like another, just like the nightly moon, and the signs and constellations seemed gradually to be fading away. I began to feel afraid that things were settling down for good like this, like a chronic illness or permanent complications, so it was better that something should happen, if only this excursion; and at the same time I was rather surprised at Leo's enthusiasm; he kept reverting to that distant day twenty-seven years before when he had lost his way and discovered that magnificent view. ('In spite of all my efforts I can't remember all the details distinctly. I remember I was wearing a coffee-coloured shirt, the one in that photo, but I can't remember which pair of trousers I had on. And good gracious me, I remember washing my legs, a lot of things I've completely forgotten, I rack my brains but can't remember them no matter how hard I try, but it's a funny thing, I remember washing my legs, though how or where I've forgotten completely.') This surprised me, and I found myself getting more and more interested in the coincidence that both of us, each in his own way, seemed similarly deeply involved in something, he in the past and I in all those trivialities.

To say nothing of the fact that my suspicions started settling on him. Might he not have had a finger in hanging the sparrow and the bit of wood? How often I had previously told myself that the idea was absurd. All the same, there was something about him. That bald, dome-like head and those pince-nez of his twitched with lewdness as well as with unhappiness, and it was a sly lewdness. He suddenly rose from the table and came back with a dried-up stick.

'It comes from there,' he announced. 'I've kept it all these years. Yes, it comes from that miraculous spot, though I'm damned if I remember where I picked it up, whether in the fields or at the side of the road.'

There he stood with his bald pate, holding the stick in his hand, and I vaguely said to myself: Stick, bit of wood, stick, bit of wood?

And that was all.

Two or three days passed like that. At last, when we took our seats in the two carriages at seven o'clock one morning, it seemed as if we were really saying good-bye. The house already looked abandoned, with the mark of approaching solitude upon it; it was to be left in charge of Katasia, who was given detailed instructions. She must take care of everything, never leave the door open, and call the neighbours if anything happened. But all these precautions applied to a situation we were about to leave behind. And so indeed we did. The two piebald horses set off down the sandy road under the indifferent dawn, the house vanished, the horses trotted, and the carriage jolted and creaked. A peasant was sitting up on the box and Louis, Lena and I were sitting on the padded seats (Leo, his wife and Fuchs were in the first carriage), and we were all still sleepy-eyed. After the house had vanished nothing was left but the motion of the carriage, rattling and creaking and jolting, and the displacement of everything all round us. But the excursion had not yet really begun. First we had to pick up one of the two young couples from their pension. The carriage jolted on. We stopped at the pension, the young couple climbed in with a lot of parcels, there was laughter and sleepy kisses were exchanged with Lena, and there was some awkward and trivial conversation.

We emerged on to the main road, the country opened out before us, and on we went. The jog-trot continued. A tree approached, passed, and disappeared behind us. A fence and a house. A small field planted with something. Sloping meadows and rounded hills. There was a break. A barrel with an advertisement on it. A car overtook us and left us behind. Our progress consisted of jolting, creaking and swaying, trotting horses, their backsides and tails, the peasant on the box and his whip, and overhead the early morning sky and the sun, which had already got boring and was beginning to burn the back of our necks. Lena jolted and swayed with the carriage, but that was unimportant, nothing was important in the slow disappearance of things that carriage travel consists of. I was absorbed by something else, something non-corporeal, that is to say the relationship between the speed with which close objects passed by and the far slower displacement of things that were not so close, to say nothing of those in the distance that seemed to be practically motionless. When one travels like this, I reflected, things appear only to disappear again, they are unimportant, and so is the landscape; there is nothing but appearance and disappearance. A tree. A field. Another tree. They passed.

I was absent. Because of our fragmentary, chaotic, casual and superficial contact with our environment we are nearly always absent, I reflected—or at any rate not entirely present. People taking part in a social occasion (such as this excursion, for instance) are about ten per cent absent, I calculated. In our case the insistent flood of things and yet more things, sights and yet more sights, this vast horizon separated by such a short distance from the restricted space in which we had been cooped up only the day before, with its involvement in clumps of earth, dust, dried-up leaves, cracks, etc. etc., warts, glasses, bottles, bits of thread, corks, etc. etc., and the configurations etc. etc., that resulted from them, became a great, dissolving stream, a deluge without end. I sank in it, and so did Lena beside me. Jolting and trotting. Snatches of sleepy conversation with the new young couple. Nothing, nothingness. Except that I was leaving the house, and Lena was with me, and Katasia had stayed behind in the house, which we were leaving farther and farther behind every moment. It, and the garden-gate and the staked and whitewashed young trees, were still there, but we were moving farther and farther away from them.

Gradually things livened up in the carriage. The newly-weds, who were called Lolo and Lola, grew more animated, and after a bout of preliminary exchanges such as 'Oh, Lolo, have I forgotten the thermos?' and 'Lola, take this bag, it's in my way,' they gave themselves up completely to lolery. Lola, who was younger than Lena, was soft and pink, had pretty dimples and pretty little fingers, a pretty little handbag and a pretty little handkerchief, as well as a pretty little sunshade, a lipstick and a lighter, and all these things kept her perpetually busy while she giggled and chatted away. 'This is the road to the Koscielisko valley, isn't it? I know it, it jolts you, doesn't it? I like it, it's a long time since I've been jolted. And you like being jolted too, don't you, Lolo? Oh, look, Lena darling. Look at that funny verandah over there, I'd have a little room for myself there, and I'd put Lolo there, where the big window is, that's where I'd give him his work room, only I'd get rid of all those little dwarfs, I can't stand little dwarfs, do you like little dwarfs, Lena? You haven't forgotten the film, have you, Lolo? Or the field-glasses? Oh, how this seat keeps sticking into my sit-upon, ow, oh dear, what are you doing, Lolo? What's the name of that mountain over there?'

Lolo was exactly like Lola, though more solid, with big calves. He was chubby and round at the hips and had a small, up-tilted nose, a small Tyrolean hat, a camera, small blue eyes, a dressing-case, plump hands, plus-fours and chequered woollen socks. They were thrilled by the practical identity of their names, and encouraged and outdid each other in their lolery. When Lola, seeing a pretty villa, for instance, announced that her mother was used to her comforts, Lolo countered by informing the world that his mother went abroad every year to take the waters, and added for good measure that she had a collection of Chinese lampshades, to which Lola replied that her mother had seven ivory elephants. It was impossible not to smile at this chatter, and our smiling encouraged them, and the chatter combined with the unreality slipping monotonously by in step with the trotting horses. Our motion resolved the landscape into concentric circles revolving at different rates depending on the distance. Louis took out his watch.

'It's half past nine.'

The sun was hot, but the air was still cool.

'Let's have a snack.'

So I was going away with Lena. This was a striking, astonishing, important fact. How on earth had I failed to realize its importance before? Everything had been left behind in the house, or outside it, such a quantity of things, from the bed to the tree and even the way we touched the spoons. And now we were here, wanderers with no fixed abode. The house with all those constellations and configurations and the rest of it was receding, was no longer 'here' but 'there', together with the sparrow in the thicket and the dappled sunshine on the black earth—a highly important fact, except that my thoughts on the subject were continually receding too—and growing weaker in the process under the impact of the surrounding landscape (though at the same time I coolly noted through half-closed eyes the curious fact that, though the sparrow was receding, its existence was by no means undermined by the process of recession, it was merely receding, and that was all).

'Where's the bread and butter?' 'Where on earth did you put the thermos?' 'Pass the paper, please.' 'Leave me alone, Lolo.' 'Where are the cups mama gave us?' 'Be careful, Lolo, don't be silly.' 'It's you that's silly, Lola.' 'Ha, ha, ha!'

What we had left behind was no longer real, but its unreality was still real. Lena's little face was small to the point of insignificance, but Louis also looked diminished, lifeless, as if annihilated by the space that extended over the barrier of a range of mountains and was terminated by another unknown range in the ultimate distance. I was ignorant of the names of most of the things around me. Those of at least half the mountains, trees, bushes, vegetables, agricultural implements, villages, etc., were completely unknown to me.

We were on a plateau.

And what was Katasia doing? Was she in the kitchen with that lip of hers? I looked at Lena's little mouth to see what it was like when freed from the intervention of that other mouth, I scrutinized its behaviour when separated from it. But there was nothing to see, it was merely a mouth on an excursion in a carriage. I ate some turkey; Kulka's provisions were delicious.

Gradually a new life established itself in the carriage, as on a new planet. Under the influence of the Lolos, Lena and even Louis began loloing too. 'What on earth are you doing, Louis?' Lena exclaimed, and he said: 'I'm not doing anything, my dear.' I watched them discreetly. It was extraordinary. So they could be like this too? A strange and incredible journey. We started dropping down from the plateau, the spaces diminished, eminences crept up on us on either side, Lena wagged her finger at Louis, and he frowned. Their gaiety was superficial and frivolous, but at any rate they were capable of it. This was interesting. But distance has its own laws and these ended by prevailing, and I ended by making a few jokes myself. After all, we were on an excursion.

Mountains which had long since been approaching were suddenly on top of us, we entered a valley where it was deliciously shady, though the foliage on the upper slopes was was still bathed in sunlight. We plunged into a quiet that came from everywhere and nowhere, a delightful river of coolness. We turned a corner, and came to towering walls and pinnacles, contorted piles of rock and deep chasms, peaceful rounded eminences, summits or peaks, craggy crests and vertical precipices to which the bushes clung, then rocks on the heights and below them meadows descending into silence, an incomprehensible, motionless, universal silence, such a powerful silence that the noise of our minute, advancing carriage seemed to exist quite apart from it. This landscape continued for some time, and then a new element imposed itself, a nude or chaotic or shining, sometimes heroic, element, made up of chasms and abysses, solid rock, variations on the theme of overhanging cliffs, ascending and descending rhythms of trees and vegetation, wounds and scars and landslides; idylls floated towards us, sometimes soft and gentle and sometimes hard and crystalline. There were all sorts of different things—marvellous distances, enchanting convolutions, space captured and stretched, aggressive or yielding space, space twisting or bending, striking up or down. Gigantic, motionless movement.

'Tremendous, isn't it, Lola?'

'Oh, Lolo, I'm frightened. I shall be frightened of sleeping alone tonight.'

Giddiness, confusion, excess. Too much, too much, too much. Weight, mass, piles rising into the sky, piles collapsed, general chaos, huge, swelling mastodons that appeared and a moment later vanished in unruly confusion into a thousand details and then suddenly reassembled again into majestic edifices. It was just as in the thicket or looking at the wall or the ceiling or the rubbish where the pole was, or in Katasia's room, or looking at the walls and cupboards and shelves and curtains where things also formed themselves into shapes and configurations. But there they had been only little things, here there was a mighty storm of matter. And I had become such a decipherer of still life that I could not help scrutinizing and examining as if there were something to be deciphered here, and I seized on the continually changing patterns that our little carriage joltingly extracted from the bosom of the mountains. But it amounted to nothing, nothing at all. A bird appeared, hovering high and motionless in the sky. Was it a vulture, an eagle, a hawk? At any rate it was not a sparrow, but its not being a sparrow made it a non-sparrow, and it was connected with the sparrow by virtue of this.

Heavens, how refreshed I was by the sight of that solitary bird hovering supremely and royally over everything, dominating the scene. It showed me how exhausted I had been by the disorder and confusion in the house down below, the chaos of mouths, the hangings, the cat, the teapot, Louis, the bit of wood, the gutter, Leo, the knockings and hammerings, the hands and the needles, Lena, the pole, Fuchs's eyes, etc., etc. I had been living in a fog. But here, heaven be praised, there was this royal bird. And by what miracle, though a mere dot in the sky, had it imposed itself like the discharge of a gun, scattering the confusion and chaos? I looked at Lena. She too was looking at the dot in the sky.

It described an arc and disappeared, plunging us back into the unbridled spectacle of the mountains, behind which there were more mountains, each consisting of spaces where stones abounded (how many stones could there be?) and thus the rear rank of that great army moved into the foreground and advanced to the assault in a strange silence, partially explained by the motionlessness of universal motion. 'Oh, Lolo, look at that rock.' 'Look over there, Lola, isn't it just like a nose?' 'Look at that old man smoking a pipe, Lolo darling.' 'Look, over there on the left, look at that top-boot, he's kicking something with it. What is it he's kicking? Oh, look, it's a chimney.' Another bend in the road restricted our vision, a balcony advanced towards us, and then a triangle, and then a tree clinging to the rock-face attracted our attention, but it promptly decomposed and disappeared. Then we saw a priest.

A priest, sitting on a stone at the roadside, wearing a cassock. A priest in a cassock sitting on a stone at the roadside in the mountains? I was reminded of the teapot, this priest was just like the teapot. His cassock was a superfluity too.

We stopped.

'Can we give you a lift, father?'

He was young and plump and had a nose like a duckling, his round, peasant's face emerged from his stiff ecclesiastical collar, and he dropped his eyes.

'May the Lord reward you,' he said.

But he did not move. His hair was clinging to his brow with perspiration. Louis asked him how far we could take him and where he would like to be dropped, but he climbed in as if he had not heard the question, muttering how grateful he was. The horses resumed their trot and we jolted on.

'I was in the mountains and lost my way,' he said.

'You're tired, father.'

'Oh, yes, I live at Zakopane.'

The bottom of his cassock was dirty, his shoes were worn, and his eyes reddish. Had he spent the night in the mountains? He explained slowly that he had been on an excursion and had got lost. An excursion in a cassock? Lost his way in an area cut through by a valley? When had he set out on this excursion? The previous afternoon. Setting out on a mountain excursion in the afternoon? We did not ask him too many questions, but invited him to help himself from our provisions, which he did. He ate with embarrassment, and when he had finished he was still embarrassed, and the carriage jolted him, the sun was scorching, there was no more shade, we were thirsty but had no desire to stop and take out the bottles, we just wanted to go on. Overhanging cliffs cast vertical shadows, and the sound of a waterfall became audible. On we went. Previously I had never taken any interest in the nevertheless remarkable fact that for centuries past a certain proportion of mankind had been set apart by wearing cassocks and being earmarked for the service of God—a whole category of specialists in the divine, servants of the spiritual, officers of the transcendental. But here in the mountains this black-clothed guest who had got involved in our trip and felt out of place in this mountain chaos was a nuisance because he was a superfluity. Rather like the teapot?

This depressed me. Curiously enough, the eagle or hawk flying high in the sky had revived my spirits, perhaps (I thought) because, being a bird, it was related to the sparrow, but also, and perhaps chiefly, because, being suspended in the sky and thus associating the sparrow with hanging, the hanged cat and the hanged sparrow . . . yes (I saw it more clearly every moment) . . . it conferred a regal, transcendental quality on the idea of hanging; and if I managed to plumb the mystery of this idea, succeeded in grasping or even suspecting what lay at the bottom of it, even if only in relation to the sparrow, the bit of wood and the cat, it would be easier for me to clear up the question of the mouths and all its ramifications. For (I went on, trying to solve the riddle, which was a difficult and painful one) there was no doubt that the secret of the link between those two mouths lay in myself, for it had arisen in me and I alone had created it. But (and here I had to watch my step, be very careful) by hanging the cat I had (completely or perhaps only to a certain extent?) associated myself with the sparrow-bit of wood configuration. Thus I belonged to both configurations. Did it not follow that the link between Lena and Katasia on the one hand and the sparrow and the bit of wood on the other existed only by virtue of my own intervention? By hanging the cat had I not in a way myself constructed a bridge connecting the whole?

No, nothing at all was very clear, but all the same something had started germinating and taking shape, and behold, a huge bird had suspended itself—had been hanging—in the sky overhead. But what the devil was this priest doing here, this totally extraneous, unexpected, superfluous, stupid priest?

He was as irrelevant, as extraneous, as the teapot had been, and I felt just as furious as when the teapot had made me kill the cat (quite right, I was by no means sure that the teapot had not been the last straw that had made me do it; also, perhaps, I had wanted to force reality to declare itself, like throwing something at a bush when you suspect something has moved in it). Yes, strangling the cat had been my furious reaction to the provocation of that senseless teapot. . . . But in that case, priest, you had better look out. For what guarantee is there that I might not fling something, do something to you . . .

He sat there quite unsuspicious of my state of mind, and on we went. Mountains and more mountains, the horses trotted on, it was stifling. A detail struck me; he was fidget-ing with his fat fingers.

He was mechanically spreading them between his knees and interlocking them; the persistence with which he kept doing this was disagreeable.

Conversation.

'Is this the first time you have been in this area?'

Lola answered like a shy schoolgirl.

'Yes, father, we're still on our honeymoon, we only got married last month.'

Lolo picked up the thread, looking just as shy and delighted.

'We're a couple of newly-weds.'

The priest coughed in embarrassment. Lola, speaking up just like a schoolgirl telling a teacher something about another girl, pointed to Lena and Louis and said:

'And so are they, father, they've just got married too.'

'They've only just had permission to . . .' Lolo announced.

Louis said 'hmm,' in a deep voice, Lena smiled, the priest remained silent, oh, those Lolos, what a way of talking they had invented especially for the priest's benefit. He went on playing miserably with his fat fingers, he was ungainly, rustic, pitiful, and it looked to me as if he perhaps had some-thing on his conscience. What was he doing with those fat fingers of his? Oh those fingers moving between his knees . . . and mine and Lena's on the tablecloth. The fork. The spoon.

'Lolo, leave me alone, what will the reverend father think?'

'Don't be silly, Lola, he won't think there's anything wrong in it at all.'

We suddenly turned, cut across the valley and started climbing the mountain, following a poor, ill-marked road. We had been in a ravine that had been growing closer and closer, and now entered another lateral ravine, and drove on surrounded by new summits and new mountainsides, and we were now completely isolated and cut off. The trees, the grass, the rocks were the same and yet quite different, marked by the obliquity and deviation that had led us away from the main road. Yes, I said to myself, he must have been up to something, he's got something on his conscience.

But what? A sin? What kind of sin? He may have strangled a cat. But how stupid can one be, since when has it been sinful to kill a cat? But this man in a cassock, this man of prayer, of the church, of the confessional, appears by the roadside and climbs into your carriage, and the immediate consequence is sinfulness, conscience, guilt and retribution, tra-la-la-la-, tra-la-la-la (which is just like tri-li-li-lee). He climbs into your carriage and you are confronted with sin.

Sinfulness, that is to say, this colleague of yours, this priest-colleague of yours, is fidgeting with his fat fingers because he has something on his conscience. Just like you. Fraternally he keeps fidgeting with his fingers. Have they too by chance strangled anything? New rock piles and chasms assaulted us, new displays of green, sombre larches and pines, a blue-green world of marvellous peace and quiet, and Lena sitting opposite me, with those hands of hers, and the whole constellation of hands—mine, hers, Louis's—had been given a shot in the arm by this fat-fingered priest's hands, which I was unable to concentrate on properly because of the motion, the mountains, the isolation. Oh, merciful, almighty God, why was it impossible to concentrate on anything? The world was a hundred million times too rich, and what could I do in my distracted state? 'Driver do you know the dance of the mountaineers?' 'Leave him alone, Lola.' 'Leave her alone, Lolo.' 'Oh, Lola, I've got pins and needles in my leg.' On we drove. One thing was clear, that bird had been too high up, and it was just as well that this priest-colleague of mine was bumbling about down here below. On we drove, the motion was monotonous, a big stream approached and passed by, the horses trotted, the carriage rattled and jolted, it was hot, we perspired, and here we were, we were just arriving.

It was two o'clock. We had reached a kind of open valley, with meadows, birds and pines. A lot of rocks were dotted about, and there was a house. A wooden house with a verandah. In the shade behind it was the gate through which Lena's parents had preceded us with Fuchs and the other young married couple. They appeared at the door, there was a babble of words, greetings and exclamations, out you

get, what a delightful trip, how long have you been here,
let's have lunch straight away, hand out the bags, it's ready
already, Leo, fetch the bottles.

They came from another planet, and so did we. Our
presence here was a presence 'elsewhere', and this house was
simply a house that was not the other house that we had
left behind.

VII

EVERYTHING was happening at a distance. It was not the other house that had left us, but we who had left it. This new house here in its terrible isolation that our cries and exclamations combated in vain had no existence of its own; it existed only to the extent that it was not the one we had left. This revelation came to me as soon as I got out of the carriage.

'We're completely on our own here, there's not a soul for miles, we're left entirely to our own resources, it's a long way to Tipperary, and we've got to fend for ourselves. What a treat you've got coming to you, all you lucky people, you'll soon see I wasn't leading you up the garden path. But the first thing to do is to stave off the pangs of hunger. Into the breach, dear friends. . . .'

'Leo, the spoons are in the rucksack. Lena, pass round the napkins, make yourselves comfortable, everyone, you, father, sit here, please.'

To which there was a chorus of replies, such as: 'We'll do as we're told,' 'good, let's sit down then,' 'we need another two chairs,' 'what a feast!' 'sit here, next to me,' 'please pass the napkins.'

The table at which we took our places was in the hall. There were a number of doors leading to the various rooms, and a staircase up to the first floor. The doors were open and the rooms more or less bare, with nothing in them but beds and chairs, a great many chairs. The table groaned with food, cheerfulness prevailed, and the wine circulated. But the cheerfulness was of the kind that prevails at parties, at which everyone behaves cheerfully in order not to spoil the pleasure of others, while the truth is that everyone feels slightly absent, as when seeing someone off at the station; and this sensation was also associated with the bareness of the house, the absence of curtains and cupboards and bedclothes or shelves and pictures on the walls; there was nothing but windows, beds and chairs.

In the emptiness not only words but personalities seemed louder, and in particular Leo and Kulka seemed to expand. Their fortissimo buzz was accompanied by the noisy voices of their guests as they ate, the giggling of the Lolos and the buffoonery of Fuchs, who was already pretty tipsy and was drinking, I knew, to drown his troubles with Drozdowski and the feeling of being unwanted, which I knew so well from my own experiences at home. He was a Jonah, poor fellow, and the only thing you could do was to shut your eyes or look away. Kulka ruled the roost, dispensing salads and cold meats, encouraging us to try just a little more of this and just a little more of that, assuring us that there was plenty to go round and that no one would have to go hungry. She had made tremendous efforts to ensure that everything was perfect and in the best of taste, she was determined to make this original excursion a social success, and she had made quite certain that there should be no excuse for anyone to complain later that there hadn't been enough to eat or drink. Leo seemed doubled or trebled in size; he was Amphitryon, guide and leader, the initiator of the whole thing, and his enthusiasm knew no bounds. 'Come children, enjoy yourselves, *carpe diem*, gather ye roses while ye may,' etc., etc. Nevertheless, in spite of all the talk and the noise, the whole thing was somehow hollow, incomplete, lacking in conviction, to such an extent that for a time I had the feeling that I was looking at my companions and myself through the wrong end of a telescope or from a great distance, as if the whole thing were happening on the moon. In other words, this excursion-evasion was useless, the world we had left was all the more present because of our attempt to get away from it. Never mind, it couldn't be helped, the only thing to do was to take things as they came. I actually had the feeling that something new was coagulating, and I began to notice little things, and in particular the peculiar excitement that overcame the Lolos in the presence of the third honeymoon couple who had arrived with Leo and Kulka.

The brand new husband was named Tolo, and was also known as the cavalry captain. Tall and broad-shouldered, with a face that was pink almost to the point of naiveté and a light moustache, he was every inch the cavalryman, and

Leo started humming a song about a dashing hussar, but broke off short, because it went on to speak of a girl who was as fresh as a rose, and the cavalry captain's bride Jadeczka was one of those resigned women who have renounced giving pleasure, having decided that such a thing is not for them, though heaven knows why. She was not unattractive, though her figure was rather uninteresting, monotonous, as it were. True, she had 'everything in the right place', as Fuchs whispered, nudging me with his elbow, but the mere thought of putting one's arm round her was unpleasing, so unsuitable was she for the purpose. Was it a kind of physical self-centredness? You felt that her hands, feet, nose, ears, were organs existing for herself alone and nothing else, she totally lacked the generosity that suggests to a woman that her hand might be a tempting and exciting gift. Was it prudishness? No, it was rather a curious kind of physical isolationism. Lola, trying hard to suppress her giggles, whispered to Lolo: 'When she smells herself she doesn't mind.' Lola was quite right, she had put her finger on why Jadeczka was so unpleasing; she was rather like those bodily smells that are tolerable only to the person who produces them.

But neither Lolo nor Lola would have been so startled, or would have had to make such efforts to suppress their giggles, if her husband had not been such a handsome, rakish-looking man with that little moustache of his. No one who saw them together could help wondering why he had married her. The answer (whispered to me with a suppressed giggle by Lola) was that she was the daughter of a rich industrialist, which of course provided further ammunition for wagging tongues. Nor was this the end of the story, indeed it was only the beginning, for (as was also evident at first sight) they had no illusions about the impression they made, and tried to counter human malice with nothing but the purity of their intentions and their perfect right to do as they pleased. Have I not a perfect right to him? she seemed to say. Of course I have. I know he is good-looking and I am not, but have I not a perfect right to be in love with him? Of course I have, and you cannot forbid me to be in love with him, for it is my unassailable human right. I love him, and my love is pure and beautiful, there is no reason why I should be bashful about it, and look, I am not. Isolated from the rest of the party and not taking part in the general hilarity, she watched over this feeling as over a treasure, concentrated and silent, her eyes fixed on her husband or lost in contemplation of the green beauty of the meadows outside the window, and from time to time her bosom heaved with a sigh that was almost a prayer. And, as was her perfect right, every now and then she quietly said something like 'Tolo', with that mouth of hers that belonged to herself alone.

Lolo said to Lola that his sides were bursting and he wouldn't be able to hold out much longer. Leo, with the leg of a turkey at the end of his fork and his pince-nez perched on his nose, held forth as usual, the priest sat in his corner, Fuchs looked for something, Kulka brought in cherries for dessert, but all the noise failed to stifle the total, singular, solitary, inhuman silence. I drank red wine.

Tolo, the cavalry captain, drank too, holding his head high. He always held his head high, to show that no one had any right to cast doubts on the genuinenesss of his love for this woman, as if he did not have a perfect right to be in love with her, as if his love for her was not as good as any other love. He was assiduous in his attentions to her. 'You're not tired, darling, are you?' he said, and he tried hard to be at the same level of ecstasy as she. But there was a slight air of martyrdom about him. 'Lolo, hold me, I can't stand it any longer.' The Lolos, wearing an air of seraphic innocence, watched and waited to pounce on the slightest sign of tenderness between them, like a couple of prowling tigers thirsty for blood. If the poor priest had given them so much pleasure in the carriage, imagine the delight they now derived from this couple, newly-weds like themselves, who seemed specially made to let them lolo to their hearts' content.

Kulka arrived with a tart. 'Oh please have some, do, it melts in your mouth, please try it. You will try it, won't you?' But the cat, oh, the cat, buried at the foot of a tree after being hanged. All this was because of the cat, the whole object of this outing was to get rid of the cat, that was why she and Leo were being so sociable. But the cat was still present, this outing was a disastrous mistake, they could not possibly have thought of anything worse. Distance wiped out nothing, on the contrary, it reinforced and strengthened it, to such an extent that it seemed as if we had spent years and years living with the sparrow and the cat and had arrived here years afterwards. I ate a slice of tart. The only thing to do was to get into the carriage and drive back, there was nothing else for it. Because if we stayed here still linked with all the things that had happened in the house. . . .

I ate my slice of tart and talked to Louis and Tolo. I was distracted. How exhausting was this superabundance and excess from which new persons, events and things constantly emerged. If only the flood would stop for a moment. Lena was sitting on the other side of the table, perhaps she was exhausted too, though she was smiling with her eyes and mouth at Lola (both of them being brides of recent date); the Lena here was a faithful reflection of the Lena there, she was 'related' to the other by a 'relationship' which now shattered me just as the hammer blows had; Fuchs was drowning Drozdowski in alcohol and was red and yellow with bloated resentment; Louis, sitting next to Lena, was quiet, agreeable and polite, and the priest in the corner. . . . Lena's hand was on the table, next to a fork, just as before, and I could have rested my hand on the table too, but I didn't want to. All the same, in spite of everything, new threads were beginning to be spun, and a new, local dynamism independent of the old was coming into being, though it seemed sickly and weak. The presence of the three young couples gave weight and significance to the priest, and the cassock in turn bestowed a marital quality on them, and the result was the creation of a sort of marital pressure; yes, marriage was dominant, the whole thing might have been a wedding reception. And then there was the priest. He kept playing with his fat fingers (which he kept under the table, withdrawing them only to take food to his lips), but nevertheless he was a priest, and as such constituted a natural bastion against the drolleries of the Lolos. Also his cassock exercised a powerful effect on Kulka, who (since the cat episode) had laid marked emphasis on the importance of correct social behaviour. Rapidly diminishing benevolence became evident in the glances she cast at the Lolos, and her disapproving little coughs became more and more expressive as Leo's outbursts of laughter grew louder and more frequent, supported as they were by Fuchs's tipsy laugh (the consequence of Drozdowski) and by our own silly jokes in the void, the distance, the deathly quiet of the mountains, in which it again seemed as if something were forming and coming into being, though it was still so vague and formless that there was nothing to fasten on yet. Meanwhile I fastened on this and that, followed whatever presented itself, neglecting all the rest, the immense, menacing rest—while all that we had left behind down in the house still existed as it had done before.

And suddenly there was a scene that connected me with the cat, through the priest.

Like the first flash of light through the dark clouds when night is over, it showed us up plainly in relation to the house below. It was preceded by remarks by Kulka of the following type. To Tolo, for instance, she said, very politely: 'Won't you remove that little bit of sugar from Jadeczka's blouse?' To Leo, in a voice intended to be heard by everyone, she said: 'It's as I said, Leo, the road isn't so bad after all, I told you we should have come by car, you should have asked Talek, he's always saying his car's at your disposal.' To Lola she said rather acidly: 'You're giggling and laughing instead of eating your tart.' Meanwhile Fuchs was removing the plates. Not being sure that he did not get on our nerves as he got on Drozdowski's, he helped with the clearing up in order to ingratiate himself. But at one point he got up, distorted his fishy, tipsy face with a yawn, and said:

'How I should love to have a bath.'

Now, baths and washing were one of Lolo's favourite topics, and Lola rated them even more highly, indeed she liked talking about them almost as much as she liked talking about her 'mama', and on the way here she had already made such statements as 'I wouldn't be able to live without a shower', and 'I don't know how anyone can live in a town without having two baths a day', and 'my mama puts lemon juice in her bath' and 'my mama goes to Karlsbad every year'. So, when Fuchs mentioned the subject, it immediately set Lola loloing. She said that if she were in the Sahara she would use her last glass of water to wash, 'because water for washing is more important than water for drinking, and wouldn't you do the same, Lolo?' etc. In the midst of all this chatter she must have noticed, as I did, that the word 'bath' was unpleasantly related to Jadeczka. Not that Jadeczka was not clean. But she had a special kind of physical self-centredness that reminded me of Fuchs's statement on another occasion that 'one is what one is.' In relationship to her own body she behaved as if (like certain smells) it were tolerable only to its owner, and consequently she created the impression of being a person uninterested in baths. Lola, after sticking out her little nose and behaving as if she could sniff something from that quarter, continued harping on the theme. 'If I miss my bath for any reason, I feel ill,' etc., etc., she said, and Lolo followed suit, and so did Leo, Fuchs, Louis, and Lena, as is usual in such circumstances, in order not to be suspected of indifference in relation to water. Jadeczka and Tolo, however, remained silent.

The result of the talkativeness on the one hand and the silence on the other was a tacit implication that Jadeczka did not take baths. Hence the feeling that 'one is what one is.'

There was a whiff coming from her direction, not a physical smell, but the whiff of an unpleasing personality; and Lola, backed up by Lolo, with the most innocent air in the world was like a bloodhound on the trail. Jadeczka, however, behaved exactly as before, that is, she remained silent and did not take part—except that her withdrawal into herself now became associated with insufficient familiarity with water; and Tolo's silence was even worse, because he was obviously a perfect swimmer and was in his element in water, so why did he not open his mouth? Did he not want to leave her alone in her silence?

'And all that business about the. . . .'

The speaker of these words moved as if he felt uncomfortable in his chair and promptly returned to his silent immobility. But this totally unexpected intervention of his had an extraordinary effect. It cut right through the loloing of the Lolos, and everyone looked at him. I don't know if we all had the same impression, but those fat fingers of his, the skin of his neck reddened by his hard collar, his physical clumsiness, the worries that he evidently had on mind and his moroseness—everything about him, in fact, including the wart at the root of his nose—connected him with Jadeczka and Jadeczka with him. His black cassock and the way he played with his fingers, her staring eyes, her self-confidence, her right to love, his awkwardness, her anguish and his suffering, combined to create a unity between them, a perfectly clear but totally unclear unity that was completely intelligible and at the same totally unintelligible. Each was stewing in his own juice and both were stewing in the same juice. 'One is what one is. . . .'

I ate some tart, but suddenly stopped with my mouth full. My throat contracted. What was I to call what was happening to me? Was it a return to the interior? A return to my own horribleness, my own dirt, my crime, my imprisonment in myself, my self-condemnation? In a flash I saw that this must lead straight back to the cat. Yes, there it was, it came creeping up, it came quite close, I could feel it. I could feel the buried, strangled cat, hanged between the sparrow and the bit of wood, all three motionless where we had left them and made significant by their very immobility. Oh, the persistent horror of it. The farther away you were the nearer they came. The more insignificant and meaningless they were, the greater their power and oppressiveness. What a diabolical noose I had put round my neck.

The cat that I had strangled and hanged.

VIII

L o u i s remarked sleepily to Lena that it would be a good
idea to have a snooze. He was perfectly right; we needed
it after starting out at dawn. We got up, and began looking
around for blankets.

'Tri-li-li-lee!'

Leo's refrain was louder than usual, and sounded provoca-
tive.

'Are you all right, Leo? Is there anything you want?'
Kulka asked in surprise.

He was sitting alone at the table, which was still loaded
with the remnants of the feast, his bald pate and pince-nez
were gleaming, and there was a drop of sweat on his brow.

'Berg!' he said.

'I beg your pardon?'

'Berg!'

'What do you mean by berg, may I ask?'

'Berg!'

There was not a shadow of benevolence about him. He
was a faun, Caesar, Bacchus, Heliogabalus, Attila. Then he
smiled mildly behind his pince-nez.

'*Nichevo*, darling, I was just going to tell a story about
two Jews who were having an argument. Never mind, I'll
tell you another time.'

It was over, disintegration had set in. The table was left
forlorn and abandoned, chairs were carried indoors, blankets
were produced, the beds in the empty rooms were occupied,
somnolence set in, the effect of the wine. . . .

At about five o'clock, when I had finished my snooze, I
walked out in front of the house.

Most of them were still asleep and no one was around. A
field with firs and pines and rocks scattered about, bathed
in sunshine and hot. Behind me the house, full of somnolence and flies. In front of me the field, and beyond it the
mountains, so many mountains, steep and wooded moun-

tains were all round. Incredible how wooded these remote places were. This was not my place, what was the point of being here? I might just as well be somewhere else, it made no difference. I knew that behind that range of mountains there were other places unknown but no more strange to me than this. A kind of indifference had interposed itself between me and the landscape, the kind of indifference that can change into rigidity or even something worse. Into what? The isolated slumber of those remote, unknown, uninteresting, rising and falling meadows and woods concealed the possibility of suddenly seizing, twisting, strangling and hanging. But the possibility was 'behind' and 'beyond', in the distance. I stood in the shadow among the trees immediately in front of the house, picking my teeth with a twig. It was still hot, but the air was fresh.

I looked round. Lena was standing five yards away.

There she was. Seeing her suddenly like this, she struck me as being small and childlike, and my eyes were attracted by her sleeveless green blouse. This lasted only for a moment. I turned my head and looked elsewhere.

'Beautiful, isn't it?'

She said this because, being only five yards away, she had to say something. I went on not looking at her, and not looking at her killed me. She had come to me, she had come to me. Did she want to start something with me? The thought terrified me, I did not look at her, and I did not know what to do, there was nothing I could do, I just stayed there not looking at her.

'So you're dumb, are you? With admiration?'

She spoke in the slightly loloish way she had picked up from them.

'Where is your father's view?' I said, for the sake of saying something. She laughed that soft, gentle laugh of hers.

'How should I know?'

Another silence, this time less embarrassing, because everything was taking place in slow motion. Heat, evening approaching, a small stone, a cockchafer, a fly, the earth. After the maximum of delay consistent with normal politeness, I said:

'Well, we shall soon find out.'

'Yes, papa's taking us after dinner,' she replied immediately.

I said nothing, but looked at the earth—at my feet. The earth and I, and she beside me. I felt uncomfortable, even bored, I should have been happier if she had gone away. Again it was time for me to break the silence, but before doing so I stole a quick glance at her, just long enough to see that she was not looking at me either, but was looking elsewhere, just as I was, and there was a touch of weakness about this exchange of non-looks, a touch of the weakness that derives from distance. Neither of us were sufficiently here, we were like projections from somewhere else, from the house we had left behind, we were weak and sickly phantoms not really here at all, like non-seeing figures in dreams who are bound up with something else. Was her mouth still 'related' to the horrible, disfigured mouth now in the kitchen or the little bedroom in that house? I wanted to find out. I took a quick glance and saw at once that her mouth and the other were related like two towns on a map or two stars in a constellation; more than ever, in fact, at this distant spot.

'What time shall we be leaving?'

'At about half past eleven, perhaps. I don't know.'

Why had I done that to her?

Why had I had to soil her like that? Why on that first night in the corridor had I first associated her mouth with Katasia's? (Alas, the things we do are as capricious and un-predictable as butterflies; it is only slowly, as one returns to them in retrospect, that they assume a convulsive quality, grip you as with pincers and do not let go.) That night it had been a fleeting idea, a caprice, a fantasy, a trifle. But now? What in the name of heaven could I do now? Now I had spoiled her for myself, spoiled her so thoroughly inside myself that I wanted to seize her and spit in her mouth. Why had I corrupted her so utterly for myself? It was worse than violating a little girl, I had violated her for myself. It was the priest's presence that suggested this to me, sinfulness was in the air, I felt I was in a state of mortal sin, which brought me back to the cat, and the cat returned.

Earth . . . clumps of earth, two clumps separated by a few

tenths of an inch. How many tenths of an inch? Two or three. I ought to go for a walk. It must be admitted that the air. . . . Another clump of earth. How many tenths of an inch?

'I had a snooze after lunch,' she said with that mouth of hers that I knew, could not fail to know, was corrupted by that other mouth.

'So did I.'

It was not she. She was down below in the house, in the garden where the little white-washed trees were tied to their stakes. I was not here either. But that made us a hundred times more significant here. As if we were symbols of ourselves. Earth. Clumps. Grass. I knew that *because of the distance* I ought to go for a walk. What was I doing standing here? I knew that *because of the distance* the significance of the here and now was immense and decisive. And this immensity. . . . Oh, that's enough, let's be off. Immensity, what sort of animal is that? The sun is setting already, what about a stroll? If I strangled and hanged the cat I ought to strangle and hang her too. It was incumbent upon me.

The sparrow was hanging in the thicket by the roadside, and the bit of wood was hanging in the crevice in the wall, they were both hanging motionless, but in the immobility here their immobility exceeded all the limits of immobility, the first limit, the second limit, the third, the fourth and fifth, and the sixth stone and seventh stone and the grass. It was getting cooler now.

I looked round, but she had gone. She had gone with that corrupt mouth of hers, and she was over there somewhere with it. I went away too, that is, I went away from the place where I was and walked across the meadow in the calm bosom of the mountains in the sunshine that was less troublesome now. My attention was absorbed by small unevennesses in the ground, but chiefly by stones lying in the grass that got in the way of my feet. What a pity that she put up no resistance to me, but how can somebody whose words serve only as an excuse for her voice put up any resistance? The way she said her piece after the killing of the cat. Ha, ha, ha. Very well, then, she doesn't put up any resistance, there will be no resistance. How painful that meeting had been, we had stood sideways without looking at each other, as if we were blind. There were more and more flowers in the grass, blue ones and yellow ones, and groups of pines and firs, the ground fell away and I was going downhill, I had gone quite a long way already, everything was inconceivably different and remote, butterflies flew about in the silence, there was a caressing breeze. Earth and grass and wooded slopes that transformed themselves into peaks. And there, under a tree, a bald patch and a pair of pince-nez. Leo.

He was sitting on a tree-trunk, smoking a cigarette.

'What are you doing here?'

'Nothing, nothing, nothing, nothing, nothing, nothing at all,' he replied, smiling happily.

'What is amusing you so much?'

'What is amusing me? Why, nothing. That's just the point. What amuses me, gentle sir and travelling companion, is precisely nothing, the nothing one does the whole of one's life. You get up, sit down, speak, write, and it's all nothing. You buy, sell, marry, don't marry, and it's all nothing. You sit on a tree-trunk and it's nothing. Like bubbles in a glass of soda water.'

He spoke slowly, casually, almost graciously.

'You speak as if you had never done any work,' I said.

'Work? And how I worked. The bank, the great big bank that keeps rumbling in my belly like a whale. Good gracious me. Thirty-two years inside the whale. And what did it all amount to? Nothing, nothing at all.'

He grew pensive and blew on his hand.

'Gone with the wind,' he said.

'What has gone with the wind?'

He replied in a nasal, monotonous voice:

'Years are divided into months, months into days, days into hours, hours into minutes and minutes into seconds, and the seconds go with the wind. They fly away and you can't catch them. What am I? An accumulation of seconds that have gone with the wind. They add up to nothing, nothing at all.

'It's downright robbery,' he exclaimed.

He removed his pince-nez and trembled with indignation. He suddenly looked old, and reminded me of the old gentleman who sometimes make speeches of protest at street corners or in the tram or outside cinemas. Ought I to say something? But what? I was lost, did not know which way to go, there were so many threads, associations, implications. Supposing I counted them all up from the beginning, the cork, the tray, the trembling hand, the chimney, no, I should get lost in a cloud of meaningless objects and other imperfectly and vaguely defined matters, one little thing kept fitting in perfectly with another like a couple of cog-wheels, and then other links leading in other directions arose, and that was what I lived on, it wasn't living at all. It was chaos, like putting my hand into a ragbag and seeing what came out and whether it was suitable . . . for building my house with, and my house assumed pretty fantastic forms. And so on *ad infinitum*. . . . And this Leo. For some time I had noted the perplexing fact that he seemed to be circling round me and sometimes even accompanying and imitating me. So there was a resemblance between us, even if it was only that he lost himself in his seconds as I did in my trivialities, and there were also other little things that provided food for thought, those bread pellets he made at dinner, for instance, and that tri-li-li-lee of his; also it occurred to me, I don't know why, that that unpleasant whiff of egocentricity ('one is what one is') that was given off by the Tolos and the priest also somehow applied to him. What harm could it do if I mentioned the sparrow and all the strange goings-on in the house? Why not mention them and see what turned up? I felt like a clairvoyant concentrating on a crystal ball.

'You're in a bit of a nervous state, and it's not surprising after all the things that have been happening during the last few days. The cat, and so on and so forth. Little things, but puzzling and difficult to shake off, like a plague of vermin.'

'The cat?' he exclaimed. 'Who gives a damn for a dead cat? Who gives a damn for a dead cat? Look at that bumblebee, old chap, what a noise it's making. Yesterday the cat tickled my nervous system, that I admit, but today, in the face of all these mountains, my divine mountains? Of course my nerves are a bit on edge, but in solemn, festival fashion. Have you not noticed, my very dear friend, have you really not noticed anything?'

'What?'

He pointed to a flower in his buttonhole.

'And please advance your honourable nose and sniff.'

Sniff? This alarmed me, perhaps more than was necessary.

'Why?' I asked.

'I am slightly perfumed.'

'You perfumed yourself for your guests?'

I sat on another tree-trunk. His baldness and pince-nez produced a glass dome effect. I asked him if he knew the names of the mountains, but no, he did not, so I asked him the name of this valley, but he said he had forgotten it.

'What do you care about the names of the mountains?' he said. 'As if that mattered.'

I was on the point of asking him what mattered, but refrained. Better let it come up of its own accord. Let the mountains do their work. When Fuchs and I reached the end of the wall and found the bit of wood we also felt as if we were at the end of the world, what with the smells, including the whiff of urine, and the heat. So what was the point of asking questions here? It would be much better to let it come up by itself, because things were undoubtedly working up to something. So I kept quiet and behaved as if I were not there.

'Tri-li-li-lee.'

I stayed perfectly still.

'Tri-li-li-lee.'

Silence, the meadow, the blue sky, the sun, which was lower now, and the lengthening shadows.

'Tri-li-li-lee.'

Each time he repeated his little refrain it came out more vigorously. By now it was positively aggressive, like the signal for an attack.

'Berg,' he then exclaimed, loudly and distinctly, in a way that made it impossible for me not to inquire what it meant.

'I beg your pardon?'

'Berg.'

'What do you mean, berg?'

'Berg.'

'Oh yes, I remember, that Jewish story. You were going to tell us a story about two Jews.'

'What story? Fiddlesticks. Berging with the berg in the berg. Don't you see? Bamberging with the bamberg. Tri-li-li-lee,' he went on in a sly tone of voice.

He moved his arms, and even his legs, as if he were dancing joyfully. Mechanically he repeated 'berg, berg,' which seemed to come up from almost unfathomable depths. Then he calmed down and waited.

'Well, I think I'll stroll on,' I said.

'No, stay where you are, why walk in the sun? It's pleasanter in the shade, much pleasanter. Such little pleasures are the best.'

'I've noticed that you like little pleasures.'

'I beg your pardon?' he said, and then he laughed with a kind of interior laugh.

'Well, I'll be damned,' he went on. 'You're perfectly right, I bet you're thinking of my little personal amusements on the tablecloth, under the eyes of my better half. My discreet little personal amusements, discreet, as is only fitting in polite society, giving no cause for comment. But she doesn't know. . . .'

'What doesn't she know?'

'That it's berging. Berging with my bamberg with all the bambergity of my bamberg.'

'Oh, I see. You have a rest here while I stroll on.'

'What's the point of dashing off like that? Wait a moment, perhaps I'll tell you. . . .'

'What?'

'What you're curious about.'

'You're a swine,' I said. 'A swine.'

Silence. Trees and shadows. A clearing. Silence. I had spoken quietly, but I had nothing to fear. At worst he would take offence and throw me out. Very well, that would be the end of that, it would cut things short, I would move to another pension or even go back to Warsaw and get on my father's nerves again and reduce my mother to despair at my insufferable character. Oh, rubbish, he would not take offence.

'You're a filthy swine,' I added.

The clearing. Silence. The only thing I was worried about was that he might be mad. For there seemed reason to fear that he might not be quite right in the head, in which case he or any possible actions or statements of his would be deprived of all significance, and this story of mine would turn out to be based on the futile and gratuitous extravagances of a poor lunatic. But by touching on this little matter of swinishness I might be able to make use of him, he might supply me with a link to Jadeczka, the priest, the cat, Katasia. He might supply another brick for the house I was laboriously building on the frontiers.

'What are you getting excited about?' he said casually.

'I'm not getting excited.'

All round us lay the peace of nature. Even if I had offended him, the whole thing was hazy and distant, as seen through a telescope.

'I might ask you by what right. . . .'

'You are utterly depraved.'

'That's enough. My lord and gentlemen of the jury, I crave your indulgence. I, Leo Wojtys, exemplary husband and father, with no police record or stain on my character, after a life-time of drudgery and toil all day and every day except Sundays and public holidays, a life-time of shuttling between my bank and my home, my home and my bank, have now retired on pension, and continue to live a no less exemplary life. Every morning I get up at 6.15 and every evening I go to bed at 11.30 (except when, by permission of my better half, I got to a little bridge party). In twenty-seven years of married life, my dear sir, I have never had another woman. In all that time I have never deceived my wife. Not once. I am an affectionate husband, kind, understanding, cheerful and polite, and I am the best of fathers. To my fellow men I am full of good will, courteous, obliging and helpful. Please tell me, my dear sir, what there is in my record that justifies you in making such . . . an insinuation, implying that I . . . surreptitiously and outside and apart from my immaculate married life . . . visit night clubs, indulge in drink, orgies, lechery, debauchery with women, bacchanalia with odalisques by lamplight. But you see for yourself that I am sitting quietly and talking and (he shouted triumphantly in my face) that I am correct in every particular and *tutti frutti*.'

Tutti frutti! The old rogue.

'You are a masturbator.'

'What? I beg your pardon? What am I to understand by that?'

'One is what one is.'

'What do you mean?'

I moved my face quite close to his and said:

'Berg.'

This worked. For a moment he swayed with astonishment at hearing this private word of his coming to him from outside. He was taken aback, and looked at me indignantly. Then he said:

'What on earth are you saying?'

But then he started shaking with inner laughter, he seemed to swell with it.

'Ha, ha, ha,' he went on. 'Berging the berg, doubly and trebly berging the berg, discreetly and surreptitiously berging the berg every moment of the night and day, and for choice at the family table in the dining-room, discreet and solitary bamberging under my wife's and daughter's eye! Berg! Berg! You have a very sharp eye, my dear sir. Nevertheless, if you will permit me. . . .'

He grew serious and thoughtful again, and then, as if he had remembered something, rummaged in his pocket and produced in the hollow of his hand a piece of sugar wrapped in paper, two or three sweets, the broken end of a fork, two indecent photographs and a lighter.

Trifles, trifles, just like the clumps of earth, the arrows, the bit of wood, the sparrow. I promptly felt positive that it had been he.

'What's all that?'

'Bergtitbits and bergpenalties awarded by the High Court. Bergpunishments inflicted by the local penal authorities and bergtitbits awarded by the department of caresses and delights. Rewards and punishments.'

'Whom do you punish and reward?'

'Whom?'

He sat there stiffly with outstretched hand, looking at it 'for himself alone', just as the priest had played with his fingers and Jadeczka found pleasure in her love . . . and just as I had corrupted my love. My fear that he would turn out to be a lunatic disappeared, it now seemed to me that we were both working together at something, working hard. Working hard at a long-term job. I wiped my brow which, incidentally, was dry.

It was hot, but by no means disagreeably so.

He moistened his fingers, carefully wiped his hand with it, and then thoughtfully scrutinized his finger-nail.

'You're cocking a snook at the world,' I said.

He made the welkin ring with his laughter, and almost started dancing without moving from his seat.

'Ha, ha, ha! Yes, you're quite right, yes, that's what I'm doing, cocking a snook at the world.'

'Did you hang the sparrow?'

'What? Hang the sparrow? Good gracious no, of course not.'

'Then who did?'

'How should I know?'

The conversation stopped short, and I did not know whether or not to revive it in this petrified landscape. I scratched off a bit of earth which was sticking to my trousers. We sat on our tree-trunks like two wise men taking counsel, though we did not know what we were taking counsel about. I again said 'berg' to him, this time more softly and quietly, and my expectations were not deceived, for he looked at me appreciatively, flicked his fingers, and murmured:

'I see that you're a berger, a bamberger, too.'

Then, in an objective, factual tone of voice, he said:

'Are you a bamberger?'

He burst out laughing and went on:

'My dear fellow, my dear fellow, do you realize why I have admitted you to the secret of my bambergery? Do you suppose I am stupid enough to admit all comers? Of course you don't. I admitted you because. . . .'

'Because of what?'

'How inquisitive you are. But I'll tell you.'

He gently took my ear and blew in it.

'I'll tell you. Why shouldn't I tell you? Well, it's because you berg, you bamberg, my own daughter, my own child and the child of my loins, by name Helena, known familiarly as Lena. You secretly and surreptitiously bamberg her. Do you suppose I have no eyes to see? You're a rogue.'

'What?'

'You're a rogue.'

'What are you getting at?'

'Still waters run deep. My dear young man, you secretly and surreptitiously bamberg my daughter, you would greatly like to creep under her skirts as berger No. 1 in her marriage. Tri-li-li-lee, tri-li-li-lee!'

The bark of a tree. Knots and veins. So he knew, or rather guessed. So my secret was out. But how much did he know? How was I to talk to him? Normally or . . . confidentially?

'Berg,' I said.

He looked at me appreciatively. A swarm, a kind of whirling bundle, of white butterflies flew across the field and disappeared behind the larches near the mountain stream. Yes, there was a mountain stream.

'So you are a bamberger, then. You're a sly one. I'm a bamberger too. We shall bamberg happily together. But all this, my dear fellow, is on the strict understanding that you keep your mouth shut, locked with a triple lock, and don't breath a word to any living soul. Because if you breathed a word to my beloved wife I'd throw you straight out of the house, head over heels, because of your evil designs on my darling daughter's marriage. I assume you accept that condition? Very well, then, in recognition of the fact that you have shown yourself to be a person worthy of confidence, it is hereby resolved that in accordance with the terms of decree . . . let us say decree No. 12,137 . . . you shall be admitted to my strictly private and secret bambergal ceremony due to take place this very day, complete with buttonhole and perfume. In other words, do you suppose, my dear sir, that I brought you all this long way just to admire the view?'

'Then why did you do it?'

'I brought you here for a celebration.'

'A celebration? Of what?'

'An anniversary.'

'Of what?'

He looked at me, and said reverently, with a kind of strange solicitude:

'Of the greatest occasion in my life. Twenty-seven years ago.'

He looked at me again, with the mystical look of a saint or martyr.

'With a cook,' he said.

'What cook?'

'The cook that was here then. The only time in my life. I carry it about inside me like the Holy Sacrament. The only time in my life.'

He relapsed into silence while I looked at the surrounding mountains. Mountains and still more mountains, rocks and still more rocks, forest and still more forest, trees and still more trees. Again he licked his finger, stroked his hand with it, and scrutinized it. Then he went on again, normally and seriously:

'You must understand that my youth was very mediocre. We lived in a small town, Sokolov, where my father was the head of a co-operative, you know what it's like in a small town, you have to watch your step all the time, everybody knows everything straight away, you know what it's like, it's like living in a glass-case, every step you take, everything you do, is public, and that's how I grew up, feeling I was being watched all the time, and on top of it, I admit, I have never been noted for outstanding courage, on the contrary, I was very shy and reserved. Of course I took a few little chances when they came my way, one does the best one can, but they didn't amount to very much. No, they amounted to very little, I was always under observation. And then, you know, as soon as I joined the bank I got married, and then there weren't many chances either, we nearly always lived in small towns, where it's like living in a glass-case with people watching you all the time and, I might even say, in those circumstances you do even more

125

watching yourself, because in marriage, you know, you watch each other from morning to night and from night to morning, and you can imagine what it was like under my wife's watchful eye, and later my daughter's. And of course at the bank you're watched all the time too. I devised a small entertainment for myself during office hours. I made a long scratch on my desk with my finger-nail, but one day the head of the department came in and said: "What on earth are you doing with your nail?" and what was I to say? The consequence was that I had increasingly to resort to minor and almost invisible little pleasures. Once, while we were living at Drohobycz, an actress came to the town on tour, she was a superb creature, absolutely superb, and one day I happened by pure chance to touch her hand in the bus, oh, what heaven, what ecstasy, oh, to be able to start life all over again, but it's no good, you can't put the clock back. I felt bitter and resentful, but I ended by pulling myself together and deciding that there was no point in wasting time thinking about touching somebody else's hand when you had two hands of your own. Believe it or not, after a certain amount of practice you can get quite expert in touching one hand with the other, under the table, for instance, where nobody can see, and even if they could see there would be nothing in it, there's nothing wrong in your hands touching or even your thighs, for example, or in touching your ear with your finger, because pleasure, it seems to me, is a question of setting your mind to it, and if you persist you can get pleasure from your own body, not a great deal of course, but it's better than nothing. I should prefer a houri or an odalisque, of course, but in the absence of a houri or an odalisque. . . .'

He rose to his feet, bowed, and sang:

> *If you can't get what you want*
> *You must want what you've got.*

He bowed again, resumed his seat, and continued:

'So I can't complain, I have managed to get something out of life. If others have managed to get more, well, good luck to them. And in any case, how can one tell? They brag and boast about the women they have had, though in reality they have had a pretty thin time. They come home, sit down, take their shoes off, and go to bed alone. So why make such a song and dance about it? At any rate I. . . . But if you concentrate on seeking out quite small and insignificant pleasures for yourself, and I do not mean only sexual pleasures, you can enjoy yourself like a pasha making little bread pellets, for instance. Or wiping your pince-nez, which I have practised for two years, because family troubles and office worries and arguing about politics are enough to drive you round the bend. I let them get on with it and just wipe my pince-nez. . . . What was I saying? Oh yes, you have no idea how these little things can help you to grow and get big. If your heel itches, it can make you feel as if you were in Volhynia at the other end of Poland, and incidentally you can get a certain amount of pleasure even from an itching heel, it all depends on your setting your mind to it. When you come to think about it, if a corn can be painful, why can it not also be pleasurable? And the same applies to sticking your tongue in the holes between your teeth. What was I going to say? Epicurism, or voluptuousness, can be of two kinds, it can be like a wild boar, a buffalo or a lion, or it can be like a flea or a mosquito, that is, it can be either large-scale or small-scale and, if the latter, it must be capable of microscopical treatment, of being divided and sub-divided and appreciated in small doses. Eating a sweet, for instance, can be divided into quite a large number of phases. First you can sniff it, then you can lick it, then you can pop it in your mouth, then you can play with it with your tongue and your saliva, then you can spit it out on to your hand and examine it, and you can burst it open with a tooth, and so on and so forth. At all events, as I have tried to make clear, you can manage without dancing, champagne, caviare, low-necked evening dress, bustling skirts, stockings, knickers, busts, ticklings, hee-hee-hee, oh, what are you doing? how do you dare? leave me alone, hee-hee-hee, ha-ha-ha, etc. I take my place quietly at the family dinner table, talk to the family and the lodgers, and nevertheless manage surreptitiously to enjoy some of the pleasures of Paris. And no one will ever find me out. No one will ever find me out. It all depends on one's creating for oneself a kind of comfortable, luxurious, voluptuous interior throne with fans and ostrich feathers in the style of Suleiman the Magnificent. Artillery salutes are important. And so is the ringing of bells.'

He rose to his feet, bowed, and again sang:

> *If you can't get what you want*
> *You must want what you've got.*

Again he bowed and resumed his seat.

'You certainly suspect me of being slightly cracked?'

'Slightly.'

'That's fine, you may assume that your suspicion is correct, it makes life easier. I play the madman to some extent to make life easier. Otherwise it would be too difficult. You like enjoying yourself?'

'Yes.'

'And you are a voluptuary?'

'Yes.'

'Well, my young friend, we are beginning to understand each other, as you see. It's really very simple. Men like . . . men like . . . what? They like love-making. They like berg.'

'Berg.'

'I beg your pardon?'

'Berg.'

'What do you mean?'

'Berg.'

'Oh, no, that's enough. Stop it.'

'Berg.'

'Ha, ha, ha, ha! So you've bamberged me. You're a deep one. You're a sly one. Who would have imagined that? You're a double, triple, superberger. That's the spirit. That's the spirit. Three cheers for berg.'

I looked at the ground. Again I found myself absorbed in the ground, the grass, and little clumps of earth. How many thousands of millions of them were there?

'Lick.'

'What?'

'Lick, I say, lickberg or spitberg.'

'*What* did you say?' I exclaimed. '*What* did you say?'

'I said lickberg or spitberg.'

The meadow, the trees, the tree-trunk. A pure chance. A pure coincidence. I must not lose my head. It was by pure chance that he had said 'spitberg', and he had said nothing about spitting in the mouth. No, I must not lose my head. He was not talking about me.

'Tonight is the great occasion.'

'What sort of occasion?'

'A pilgrimage.'

'You're very pious,' I remarked, and he looked at me with the same strange solicitude as before, and said earnestly and shyly:

'How could I not be pious? Of course I'm pious. Piety is essential, indispensable, the *sine qua non*. Not even the slightest of little pleasures can be enjoyed without piety. Oh, what am I saying? Personally I know nothing about it, and sometimes I'm lost as in a vast cloister, but you must appreciate that piety is the secret rule of the order, the holy mass on which the whole thing depends. Amen, amen, amen.'

He rose, bowed, and said:

'*Ite missa est.*'

Then he bowed again and sat down.

'The whole point,' he went on in an objective, matter-of-fact way, 'is that Leo Wojtys enjoyed pleasure, that is to say, absolute, perfect pleasure, only once in the course of his grey life, and that was twenty-seven years ago with the cook who worked in this mountain refuge. That was twenty-seven years ago. Today is the anniversary. Actually it is not the real anniversary, it's a month and three days short. And they (he leaned towards me as he said this) think I brought them here to admire the view. Actually I brought them here on a pilgrimage to the spot where twenty-seven years ago less one month and three days, I . . . that cook. I brought them here on a pilgrimage. My wife, my daughter, my son-in-law, the priest, the Lolos and the Tolos, are all here on a pilgrimage in honour of my supreme experience, my superberg, and at midnight I shall emberg them to the place below the rock where she and I. . . . Let them commemorate the occasion. Unknowing pilgrims to the voluptaberg. But *you* will be in the secret.'

He smiled.

'But you will not tell.'

He smiled again.

'Do you bamberg?' he said. 'So do I. We shall bamberg together.'

Again he smiled.

'Now go,' he went on. 'I want to be alone, to concentrate my mind and prepare myself with due reverence for my solemn mass, my celebration, my greatest celebration. I want to be alone, so that in fasting and prayer I may purify and prepare myself to celebrate the memory of the most divine bamberg of my life on that unforgettable day. Now go, *arrivederci*.'

The fields, the trees, the mountains, the sky and the declining sun.

'And don't imagine that I'm gaga. I merely play the fool to make things easier. In reality I am a monk and a bishop. What is the time?'

'It's past six.'

His mention of spitting had of course been sheer coincidence. How could he possibly know anything about Lena's mouth that I carried about inside me? But these curious coincidences were more frequent than one would have expected, things kept popping up and sticking together as if they were glued, events and happenings were like those magnetized particles that sought each other out and joined up with one another as soon as they got close enough, never mind how. There was nothing surprising in his having discovered my secret passion for Lena, he was certainly a specialist in these things. And was it he who had hanged the sparrow and was responsible for the arrow and the bit of wood, as well as the pole, perhaps? Probably. No, certainly. But it was immaterial, it made not the slightest difference whether it was he or another. The really curious and interesting thing was that the sparrow and the bit of wood were still present and had not lost one iota of their power. Was there no salvation anywhere? It was also very curious and interesting that there should be this resemblance between us that made us click like two cog-wheels. In some things it was very obvious, as in his worship of details. Did we really have something in common? But what? Could it not be said that he was escorting me, guiding me, leading me astray? Sometimes I had the feeling that I was co-operating with him in a difficult birth—as if both of us were giving birth to something. Oh, come, come. Alternatively (how many alternatives can there be?) there was the consideration that 'one is what one is' that could not be overlooked. Might not that be the clue to the riddle of what was cooking here? A kind of growing wave approached me from that quarter, that of the priest and the Tolos, and it contained a menace, and the menace approached me like a forest, yes a forest—we say 'forest', but think what it means, think how many little details and particles go to make up a single leaf of a single tree, we say 'forest', but the word implies the unknown, the inconceivable, the unknowable. Earth and stones. You rest in broad daylight among ordinary, every day things that have been familiar since childhood; grass, trees, a dog (or cat), a chair, but only so long as you do not realize that each and every object is a huge army, an inexhaustible host. I was sitting on my tree-trunk as on a suit-case, waiting for a train.

'Tonight's pilgrimage will be to the place of my unique and supreme bliss experienced twenty-seven years ago, less one month and three days.'

I rose to my feet, but he was obviously unwilling to let me go without more definite information, he started talking more quickly, the words came pouring out of him.

'Tonight the secret and occult celebration of the great bambergus is taking place,' he said. 'The view? What view? You are all here to celebrate the anniversary of my supreme bambergus with the cook I told you about who used to work at the house,' he called out as I walked away. Fields, trees, mountains, vulture-like shadows.

I walked on. The grass was yellow and fragrant, flowers were dotted about, the fragrance was not like that by the wall which Fuchs and I had reached by following the direction of the broom-handle after crossing the area of whitewashed trees tied to their stakes and the waste area covered with weeds and rubbish. There had been a smell of urine, or whatever it was in that urine-like warmth, and the bit of wood had been waiting for us in that warm and disagreeable fragrance, waiting to be associated, not immediately, but later, with the pole lying in the rubbish in the hut, the harness and other odds and ends, and the door had been open.

The pole had led us to Katasia's room—the kitchen, the key, the window, the ivy—and all the things hidden all over the place had reached a climax in Kulka's hammering and Lena's knocking, which had led me to the big, prickly pine-tree I had climbed, and then I had seen the teapot, which had led to my murderous assault on the cat. The cat, the cat. How disgusting, it's enough to make you sick, I said to myself drowsily, the field was drowsy, and I walked on slowly, staring at the ground beneath my feet and looking at the flowers, and suddenly I fell into a trap.

It was a stupid, trivial trap. In front of me were two small stones, one to the right and the other to the left. On the left a little farther on there was a brown patch of earth that had been loosened by ants, and beyond that, also on the left, there was a big, black, rotten root, and these three things were in a straight line, hidden in the sunshine, sewn up in it, concealed in the luminous air. Just when I was on the point of walking between the two stones I made a small diversion to pass between one of them and the little patch of earth that the ants had turned over, it was a minimal diversion amounting to nothing at all, but there was no real reason for it, and that, I think, disconcerted me. So I mechanically made another minor diversion to pass between the two stones as I had originally intended, but I experienced a certain difficulty about this, a very slight difficulty, it is true, deriving from the fact that in view of these two successive diversions my intention to pass between the stones had assumed the quality of a decision, a trivial decision, needless to say, but nevertheless a decision. There was no excuse for this, of course, for the total neutrality of the objects lying in the grass justified no decision. What difference did it make which way I went? Also the valley, sleeping in its covering of trees, dazed by the buzzing of flies, seemed petrified, embalmed. Silence, drowsiness, sleep, dreams. In these circumstances I decided to pass between the two stones. But the few moments that had passed made the decision more of a decision than ever, and how was one to decide since it made no difference either way? So I stopped again. Furious at this, I again put my foot forward to pass between the stone and the patch of earth, as I had now decided, but realized that if I did so after two false starts it would not be ordinary walking, but something more important. So I decided to take the route between the patch of earth and the root. But then I realized that if I did this I should be acting as if I were afraid, so again I decided to pass between the stone and the patch of earth. Good heavens alive, what was happening, what was the matter with me, I could not allow myself to be held up like this on a level path while I struggled with such phantoms. What was the matter with me? The vegetation, the flowers, the mountains were enveloped in a warm, gentle drowsiness, and not even a blade of grass moved. I did not move either, I just stood. This position became more and more irresponsible and actually crazy. I had no right to stand there like this, it was impossible, I must go on, but I stayed rooted to the spot. And then, in the general immobility my own immobility became identified with that of the sparrow in the thicket and all the things that were immobile down there below, the sparrow, the bit of wood, the cat, and the death-like immobility that was accumulating here. At this I moved, thereby immediately destroying all the impossibility inside me, and I moved forward quite easily, without even realizing which way I was going, because it was completely immaterial, thinking about something else as I did so, namely, that the sun disappeared earlier here, because of the mountains. Yes, the sun was already pretty low. I walked on towards the house, whistling to myself, I lit a cigarette, and all that was left in my mind was a vague residue, a pale memory.

There was the house. No one was around. The windows and doors were wide open, the place was empty. I lay on a bed and rested. Later, when I went downstairs again, Kulka was in the hall.

'Where are they all?' I said.

'They've gone for a walk. Would you like some punch?'

IX

S H E gave me the drink and silence fell. It was a sad, or tired, or resigned silence. Neither of us concealed from the other that we had no wish to speak, or could not. I drank slowly, in long gulps, and she leaned out of the window, looking exhausted, as if after a route march.

'Mr Witol,' she said, without pronouncing the final 'd', as she did when she was nervy. 'Have you ever seen such a hussy? She can't even leave a priest alone. What does she take me for? A brothel madam?' (she suddenly shrieked, completely beside herself). 'I won't stand for it. I'll teach them to behave themselves when they are in polite society. And that husband of hers, that little whippersnapper in plus-fours, is even worse. If she were the only one to be-have like that it would be bad enough, but he carries on just like she does. Have you ever seen one man provoking another with his own wife? It's absolutely incredible, making her sit on his knees, just imagine a husband flinging his wife at another man, and on his honeymoon, too. I should never have believed that a daughter of mine would have such immoral and mannerless friends. And it's all aimed at Jadeczka, they're trying to spoil her honeymoon. I've seen a great many things in my life, Mr Witol, but I've never seen anything like that, and I won't stand for it.' Then she said:

'Have you seen Leo?'

'Yes, I met him, he was sitting on a tree-trunk.'

I slowly emptied my glass and waited for her to go on, and I wanted to say something myself. But she didn't want to go on, and I ended by not wanting to say anything either. Impotence. What was the good of talking? We were too far away, over the hills and valleys, we were elsewhere.

But even this was an absent feeling, not really felt, so to speak. I put down my glass, said something, and walked out.

This time I strolled off in the opposite direction. I was

looking for them. With my hands in my pockets and bent head, thinking with the deepest part of my being but without a real thought in my head—as if all my thoughts had been stolen from me. The valley, with its plumes of trees, its mantles of forests, the mountainous humps all round, attracted my attention, but in the background, so to speak, like a noise, the sound of a distant waterfall, an incident from the Old Testament, or the light of a star. In front of me were millions of blades of grass. I raised my head, for loloish laughter and giggles reached my ears, and they emerged from behind the trees. 'Lolo, stop it at once.' 'Lola, let go or I'll bite.' Blouses, shawls, handkerchiefs, plus-fours. They were advancing in disorderly fashion, and when they saw me they waved, and I waved too.

'Where have you been? What have you been up to? We've been all the way to that hill over there.'

I joined them, and walked straight in the direction of the sun, which had now vanished. All it had left behind was a solar void, a kind of sunny emptiness exposed by the tense brilliance coming from behind a mountain as from a hidden source and inflaming the lilac sky that was now shining as if for itself and was no longer in communication with the earth. I looked round. Down below everything had changed, though it was still daylight. But the beginnings of a kind of indifference had set in, a kind of condensation and a sense of abandonment, as if a key had been turned in a lock. The mountains, hills, stones, trees, now existed only for themselves and were approaching their end. The gaiety of our little party was cacophonous, like the sound of a breaking window-pane. Nobody walked with anyone else, everyone was on his own. The Lolos were on the flank, she in front and he behind, looking cheerful, though you could tell that all was not so gay within. The main body consisted of Lena, Louis and Fuchs. Tolo and Jadeczka were on the other flank, with the priest behind them. But they were scattered all over the pace. There are too many, what am I to do with them? I said to myself in alarm.

I was amazed to see Fuchs skipping about in a state of huge delight and calling out:

'Help! Help! Help me, Miss Wojtys, please!'

'Don't you dare help him, Lena, he isn't on his honeymoon,' said Lola.

'I'm always on honeymoon, I'm on permanent honeymoon,' said Fuchs.

'It happens to him every month,' said Lolo. 'He's always going on about what happens to him monthly.'

Lena laughed softly.

Oh, the honey, the sticky honey of that triple honeymoon. In Jadeczka's case it turned into a private and peculiar honey of her own, because when she smelled herself she didn't mind and she did not take baths, why should she, or if she did it was only for hygienic reasons, for herself alone and not for anyone else. The Lolos were going for Fuchs, but of course Jadeczka was their real target, Fuchs was only the cushion off which the billiard balls bounced, and he knew it, but he was delighted at being bombarded with their jokes; he, Drozdowski's victim, was tickled to death and was almost dancing with red-haired ecstasy. While he thus danced for himself alone in close proximity to the Lolos a deep and rather repellent silence prevailed on the part of the Tolos. At my feet there was grass and yet more grass, made up of stalks and leaves in various positions and at various angles, twisted or broken, crushed or dried up; this fleetingly caught my attention, which was chiefly engaged by the whole of the vegetation which extended uninterruptedly to the mountains but was already locked up and condemned to itself.

We advanced slowly. Fuchs's laughter was even more stupid that the Lolos' giggles. I was taken aback by his idiocy, the surprising crescendo of his idiocy, but even more by the honey which was increasing and multiplying. It had started with the talk about honeymooning, but now, thanks to Jadeczka, it became more and more 'private' and disgusting. And the priest contributed to this by his insistent twiddling with his fingers. This amorous and disgusting honey was also connected in some way with me. Oh, these connections. I must stop connecting and associating.

Our slow, wandering footsteps led us to an idyllic little stream. Fuchs hurried forward, sought out the easiest place to cross, and called out 'this way'. Lack of light increasingly impinged on the light framed by the trees on the mountain-side. Lola called out:

'Lolo, please carry me across. Take pity on my shoes, Lolo, please. Please carry me across, darling.'

'Tolo, you carry her across,' Lolo said impudently.

Tolo's reply took the form of a cough, whereupon Lolo wriggled his hips and said with an innocent, schoolboy air:

'You will oblige me, won't you, Tolo, I'm dead beat, I've no strength left.'

The subsequent course of events was as follows. Lola called Lolo a weakling and a coward and dashed over to Tolo and started what was almost a little dance in front of him.

'Please take pity on me, Mr Tolo,' she said. 'Look, my husband has let me down, please take pity on my poor shoes.' And she held out her little foot.

'Come on, Tolo, one, two, three and it's done. Where's your courage, man?' said Lolo, and Lola said 'one, two, three,' and tried to put herself in his arms.

'Come on, one, two, three and it's done,' said Lolo.

I did not take too much notice of all this, for I was more or less absorbed by the scene that enveloped us, the surrounding mountains that from a distance embraced and enclosed us. There was a certain severity about them now, for their covering of forests made them grimmer as darkness fell (high above us there was still bright light, though it was separated from us). But I distinctly saw the Lolos dancing a war dance, the cavalry captain not doing so, Fuchs in the seventh heaven of delight, Louis not in the seventh heaven of delight, the priest standing still, and Lena. . . . Oh, why had I contaminated her with Katasia's lip on that first night in the corridor, and why, instead of forgetting it next day, had I returned to it and made the contamination permanent? There was one thing I was curious about: had that association been pure caprice on my part, or had I divined a real link between that mouth and that lip? But what link? What link?

Had it been pure caprice and fantasy? No. I felt no guilt in the matter. It had come to me, not from me. And why should I have deliberately made her repulsive to me, since without her my life would henceforth be meaningless and grey, spoilt and disfigured? There she stood, looking so attractive that I looked the other way, preferring to stare at the grass and have the valley in my head. No, the situation was not that that filthy association with Katasia prevented me from loving her, it was far worse than that. I did not want to love her, I simply did not want to, and the reason was that if my body had been covered all over with spots and in that state I had set eyes on Venus herself, I should not have wanted her either. I should not have looked at her. I felt ill, so I did not want her. But have a care, have a care. So it was I who was disgusting and not she? So I was the source of the disgust, it was my fault? I could not make head or tail of it and never would. But look.

'Come on, man, be bold.' Lolo's calves covered with chequered socks. 'Come on, carry her across, you're on honeymoon too.'

Then came Jadeczka's deep, confident, generous voice:

'Please carry the lady across, Tolo,' she said.

I looked. By this time Tolo was depositing Lola on the grass on the other side of the stream, and the farce was over. We resumed our progress, our slow progress over the grass. Honey, why honey, why honey? Why did I connect honey with the priest's fingers? I walked on as if in the middle of a wood at night, when noises, shadows and fugitive, intangible shapes surround and oppress you, always on the point of assaulting you. . . . And Leo with his bamberging in the berg? When and from where would the prowling wild beast pounce? The mountain-ringed meadows led straight to silence, abandonment and isolation, to pockets of non-existence and invisibility, to citadels of blindness and dumbness, and behind some trees in their midst there appeared the house that was not a house, the house that existed only to the extent that it did not exist, was not that other house with its self-contained system of hanged sparrow, bit of wood, and cat, the whole supervised by the disfigured mouth of Katasia, who was in the kitchen—or the garden—or perhaps out on the verandah.

The penetration of this house by the other was not only troublesome, it was also morbid, completely and horribly morbid, and not only morbid but also imperious, and I said to myself oh well, it can't be helped, there's nothing that can be done about it, the whole constellation can no longer be destroyed or got rid of, there's no getting away from it, it's too well established by now and there's too much of it. And I walked on mechanically, and Louis asked me if I could lend him a razor-blade (but of course, with pleasure), and I said to myself that nothing could be done about it, because any attempt to fight it off or run away from it only embroiled your further, as in one of those traps in which the slightest movement only ensnares you more deeply. And who knows, perhaps this had happened to me only because I had defended myself against it. Perhaps I had been too frightened when Katasia's lip first mingled in my mind with Lena's, and perhaps that had caused the seizure with which it had all begun. Might my defence have preceded the attack? I could not tell. In any case it was too late now. A polyp had formed somewhere on the surface of my being, and the more I destroyed it the more obstinately it survived.

The house in front of us seemed already to have been ravaged by the dusk, and its very substance had been weakened. The whole valley was filled with helplessness, the sky was vanishing, curtains of mist were being drawn across it, things were refusing to communicate and were creeping back into their lairs. They were disappearing, disintegrating, coming to an end. It was still fairly light, but the power of sight itself seemed to be dangerously diminishing. I smiled, saying to myself that darkness was propitious, in the dark one could approach, touch, seize, embrace, make love to the point of madness, but what was the use, I did not want to, I was ill, I had a rash, I was ill. All I wanted was to spit in her mouth.

I did not want to.

'Look.'

I heard the woman say this quietly but fervently to her loved one (and without looking at them I was sure she was referring to the lilac-coloured horizon). 'Look,' she said in a sincere and elevated tone with her buccal orifice, and I also heard him reply 'yes' in a deep voice that was no less sincere. And what about the priest? What was he up to with those fingers of his?

When we got close to the house Fuchs and Lolo ran a race to the front door.

We went in. Kulka was in the kitchen. Leo emerged from one of the other rooms with a towel in his hands.

'Get ready for supper, children,' he said. 'Make yourselves neat and tidy, all nice and shiny like a packet of new pins. A bite will do you good after your walk.'

Louis again asked me to lend him a razor-blade, and immediately afterwards Leo nudged me and asked if he could borrow my watch, because he could not rely on his own. I gave it to him, and asked him whether punctuality was so important, and he whispered that it had to be exact to the very minute. Soon afterwards Louis came back and this time asked me if I could lend him a piece of string, but I had none. A watch, a razor-blade and a piece of string, I said to myself. They kept asking for things, what was cooking now? How many plots were hatching simultaneously with my own? How many non-apparent, rudimentary, distorted or concealed configurations were maturing independently of my own? And what was that priest up to, for instance?

The table was already half laid, the shadows in the house were growing blacker, night prevailed on the staircase, but in our room on the first floor, where Fuchs was combing his hair in front of a pocket mirror on the window-ledge some light still remained. Nevertheless the darkness of the forests covering the slopes about a mile away crept in through the window in hostile fashion, and two trees near the house started rustling, for a breeze had sprung up.

'It was absolutely fantastic, old man.' Fuchs was talking. 'It was absolutely fantastic, I tell you. You saw for yourself how they had it in for those two, but you can't imagine what it was like during the walk. It was enough to make you split your sides, when once they get their knives into someone, heaven preserve him. But I must admit I'm not surprised. The worst of it is that Lola is so . . . inspired, that's the only word for it. Would you mind holding the comb for me? Thank you. Actually I can't blame Lola. Jadeczka's buying herself a husband with her father's money is provoking enough, but running after another man on top of it. . . . Of course it's embarrassing for Lena, because they are her guests and both of them are friends of hers, and she hasn't enough savoir-faire to handle the situation, she's too weak, and Louis is a strange fellow, he's nothing but a well-dressed office work-horse, he doesn't amount to anything at all, I wonder why Lena picked on a man like that, it's extra-ordinary the choices people make. Of course it's a difficult situation with three honeymoon couples, and trouble was to be expected, after all. But I must admit that going too far is going too far, and I can't blame Lola for wanting to get her own back. She actually caught her in the act with Lolo.'

'What do you mean, caught her in the act?'

'I saw it with my own eyes. At lunch, when I bent down to pick up a box of matches. His hand was on his knee under the table, and Jadeczka's was just beside it, only a fraction of an inch away, and not in a very natural position either. You can guess the rest.'

'You must have imagined it.'

'Imagined it? I certainly did not imagine it. I've got a nose for that sort of thing. And Lola must have noticed it too, I could tell from her behaviour. Now both she and Lolo have got their knives into Jadeczka.'

I did not want to argue, it was too much for me. Was it possible? Why should it not be possible? Jadeczka might be like that, why should she not be like that? If she were, thousands of reasons could be found to explain it. But why should Fuchs not have been mistaken? Perhaps he had not seen properly, he might have been mistaken, or he might even have invented the whole thing for reasons of his own. I was ill, ill, ill; and the fact that *hands* had turned up again alarmed and oppressed me and made me clench my fingers. How many dangers threatened. Meanwhile Fuchs went on talking, changed his shirt, showed his red face, talked red-facedly, the sky faded into nothing, Leo could be heard singing *She's just the girl for dad*, and I said cruelly:

'And how about Drozdowski?'

He flushed.

'Good God, man, how brutal can one be?' he exclaimed. 'Do you have to remind me of him now? When I think that in a few days' time I'll be cooped up with him again for seven hours a day . . . he makes me sick, I tell you, it's incredible the knack he has for getting on my nerves. If you could only see the way he has of sticking out his leg. It's enough to make you feel sick. But to hell with him, *carpe diem*, gather ye rosebuds while ye may, as Leo says, I'm going to enjoy myself while I can, am I right or not?'

From down below Kulka could be heard announcing in a wooden, if not actually stony, voice that supper was ready. The wall beside the window facing me was rich in distractions, as all walls are; there were veins, a round red patch, two scratches, the paper was peeling in one or two places and some of the fibre was in a bad state, it was the accumulation of years. In fact not much of the paper was left, but it was still there, and as I found my way about it I said I wondered what the latest news of Katasia was and whether anything had happened down at the house, what did he think? I stopped for a moment listening to my own question.

'What on earth do you expect to have happened? Do you really want to know what I think? Well, I'll tell you. If we hadn't been so bored there, nothing at all would have happened. Boredom, my dear fellow, makes you imagine even more things than fear does. Heaven alone knows what you're capable of imagining when you're bored. Come on.'

Down below it was dark, and above all it was cramped. The hall was uncomfortable, and the table had had to be put in a corner because of two benches that were fixed into the wall. Several persons were engaged in taking their seats on them, to the accompaniment of jokes and laughter, of course. 'A squeeze in the dark. What could be more ideal for honeymoon couples?' somebody said, whereupon Kulka brought in two petrol lamps that spread a sort of foggy light.

A moment later, when one had been put on a shelf and the other on a cupboard, they burned better, and the oblique light they cast magnified our bodies ranged round the table and made them fantastic; vast shadows swept along the wall, the light cruelly revealed fragments of faces and busts while the rest was invisible, more people took their seats, making it more cramped than ever, it was like being in a dense forest,

and the enlargement of hands, sleeves and necks made it
denser still. Meat was served, vodka was poured out, and the
whole thing was like a phantasmagoria of mastodons and
hippopotami. The lamps made the darkness outside denser
and wilder than before. I sat next to Lola. Lena was rather
a long way away between Jadeczka and Fuchs on the other
side of the table. In this fantastic scene heads joined up with
each other and hands outstretched towards dishes projected
complicated shadows that mingled with each other on the
walls. There was no lack of appetite, people helped themselves to ham, veal and beef, and the mustard circulated. I
had a good appetite myself, but the thought of spitting in
her mouth . . . the food in my mouth got covered with
spittle. And honey. My appetite was poisoned and so was I.
Jadeczka, in ecstasy, let Tolo give her a second helping of
salad and I wondered whether it was possible that she might
be not only what I thought she was, but also what Fuchs
said she was. It was by no means impossible, with that buccal
orifice of hers and the state of ecstasy she was in she might
really be like that, for everything was always possible, and
among the thousands of millions of possible reasons for everything you could always find one to explain anything. And
the priest? What was the truth about this silent priest who
was swallowing something just as if it were noodles or
porridge? He ate awkwardly, his way of ingesting food was
peasant-like, poor and pinched, somehow downtrodden like
a worm (though I couldn't really say for certain, I wasn't
sure about anything, I was staring at the ceiling). But what
was the matter with him? Was something cooking in that
quarter? I too did the meal pretty good justice, though I
was nauseated. But it was I who was nauseating, not the cold
veal, what a pity to have to spoil . . . everything by my own
corruption. But I was not too upset by this, for what could
really upset me at this distance? Leo was also eating at a
distance. He was sitting right in the corner, where the two
fixed benches joined, the protruding lenses of his pince-nez
shone like drops of water under the dome of his bald pate,
his face was suspended over his plate, and he cut some bread
and ham into small pieces, and then proceeded as follows:
he stuck his fork into each morsel, raised it to his mouth,

popped it in, tasted it, masticated it, and finally swallowed it; consequently he took a long time over each. Strangely enough, he was silent, and perhaps for that reason there was little conversation, everyone just ate. Leo obtained satisfaction by eating like that, it was a kind of masturbation, and I found this pretty wearing, particularly as the way Jadeczka was satisfying her appetite next to the cavalry captain, though dissimilar, was similar ('one is what one is'); and, apart from the way she ate, there was also the way the priest ate, which was rustic. And 'eating' was connected with 'mouths', and in spite of everything mouths started haunting me again. Spitting in her mouth. Spitting in her mouth. I went on eating, not without appetite, which disgustingly enough testified to the fact that I had got used to my own spit, but I was not disgusted by my disgust, for it was distant.

I went on eating cold veal and salad. There was also vodka.

'The eleventh.'

'The eleventh is a Tuesday.'

'. . . with silver plate at the bottom it's all right.'

'. . . to the Red Cross, but they said that. . . .'

Snatches of conversation. '. . . or nuts, the salted ones.' 'I won't take no thank you for an answer. Take some more and don't argue.' 'He sticks to the right and won't let anyone pass.' 'Whose?' 'Last night.' The forest grew thicker, and seemed to be going round and round. I was in the middle of a cloud that was also going round and round and was always bringing up something new, so much of it that it was impossible to remember and grasp it all. It had all begun with the iron bed on which she had been lying when I first saw her and noticed her foot, but in the meantime that bed seemed to have got lost somewhere on the way. And the bit of cork in the dining-room had also vanished. And then there had been the knocking noise and the chicken Louis had talked about, and the ashtray, and the staircase, yes, the staircase, and the little window, the chimney and the gutter, and all the rubbish lying under and round the pole, and of course the fork, the knife and the hand, the hands, her hand, my hand, Leo's tri-li-li-lee, to say nothing of Fuchs and all the rest of it, for instance the ray of sunshine coming in through a crack in the blind, and our following the direction indicated by the broom-handle, and the staked trees, and our tramp along the road in the heat. Oh Lord, oh Lord, the exhaustion, the smells, the cup of tea . . . and the way Kulka said 'my daughter' and, oh Lord in heaven above, the hole behind that root and so on and so forth, and that bit of soap in Katasia's room, and the teapot, and her fugitive glances as modest as a sprig of mimosa, the garden gate and all its details, including the padlock, oh almighty and merciful God, all the things on the window-sill and under the ivy, and when the light went out in their room, the branches of the pine-tree when I climbed down, and the priest on the road, and the prolongation of those imaginary lines, oh Lord, oh Lord, the bird hanging in the sky, Fuchs taking off his shoes and conducting his stupid inquest in the dining-room, and the way we had left the house in Katasia's charge, the verandah and the door when we first set eyes on it, the heat, the fact of Louis's going to his office and the situation of the kitchen in relation to the house, one particular stone, a yellowish one, and the key to Katasia's room, the frog— what on earth had happened to that frog?—a bit of ceiling that was peeling, and the ants near the second tree along the path, and the corner of the house behind which we were standing when . . . oh Lord, oh Lord, oh Lord, *Kyrie eleison*, *Christe eleison*, the tree on the height over there, and that place behind the cupboard, and my father and my rows with him, the wire on that hot fence, *Kyrie eleison*. . . .

Leo put a bit of salt on his finger, raised it to his mouth, put it on his tongue, and then withdrew it.

'. . . they were forced sideways on top of them'. . . . 'somewhere in the Bystra neighbourhood'. . . . 'on the second floor, I wonder if anyone'. . . . Words accumulating as on a dirty carpet . . . or ceiling.

Leo finished eating and sat there with his face concealed under his dome-like head. His face seemed to be suspended from his bald pate. . . . No doubt the reason why they were talking so much was that he was silent. His silence created a gap.

He dabbed his finger on a little pile of salt to make some stick to it, inspected his finger, put out his tongue, put the salt on it, closed his mouth and savoured it.

Jadeczka took some slices of cucumber with her fork. She was silent.

The priest leaned forward with his hands under the table. His cassock.

Lena, who had been sitting there quietly, suddenly engaged in a whole series of minor activities. She folded her napkin, moved a glass, removed a speck of dust, put a glass in front of Fuchs, and smiled.

Lolo jumped to his feet and called out: 'Bang!'

Kulka came in, stood there stolidly for a moment, looked at the table, and withdrew to the kitchen again.

Why did I notice these things and not others? Why? I looked at the walls. Dots and stains. Something emerged from them, a kind of shape, but it vanished, leaving chaos and excess behind. What was the matter with the priest? And with Fuchs, Jadeczka and honey. And where was Louis (he wasn't there, he had not come down to supper, I assumed he was shaving, I wanted to ask Lena where he was, but didn't). And what had become of the peasants who had driven us here? Chaos and confusion. What can one know? Suddenly I was struck by the landscape outside, the landscape with all its variations stretching to the mountains and beyond, the main road winding through the night, which was painful and oppressive. Why had I strangled the cat? Why had I strangled the cat?

Leo raised his eyes and looked at me very thoughtfully and attentively and even laboriously—and helped himself to a glass of wine and raised it to his mouth.

His attentiveness and laboriousness communicated themselves to me. I raised my glass to my mouth and drank.

His eyebrows were quivering. I dropped my eyes.

'Ladies and gentlemen, I ask you to rise and drink to the health of the bachelors'. . . . 'Shame on you, how dare you propose that toast on your honeymoon!'. . . . 'Well then, the ex-bachelors'. . . . 'Leave him alone, let him drown his sorrows'. . . . 'What *are* you doing, Lolo?'. . . . 'What are *you* doing, Lola?'

Leo, with pince-nez gleaming under his bald pate, stretched out his finger, took a pinch of salt, popped it in his mouth and kept it there.

Jadeczka raised her glass to her lips.

The priest produced a very strange sound indeed, a kind of glug-glug. He shifted in his seat.

A small window, with a little hook.

I took a long drink.

Leo's eyelids were quivering.

I dropped my eyes.

'Why are you so thoughtful, Mr Wojtys?'

'Mr Wojtys, what are you thinking about?'

This was the Lolos. Then Kulka said:

'Leo, what are you thinking about?'

She asked the question fiercely, standing in the kitchen doorway with dangling hands, and she made no attempt to conceal her anxiety; she spoke as if she were injecting anxiety into us with a syringe, and I thought hard and deeply and at the same time my mind was a blank.

'She asks what I'm thinking about,' said Leo casually, as if the question had nothing to do with him.

Honey.

The tip of his tongue appeared between the slit of his thin, pink lips and stayed there, it was the tongue of an old gentleman in pince-nez. Tongue, spitting in her mouth, then suddenly a scene of chaos and confusion that was like thunder and lightning, and Lena's mouth and Katasia's came to the surface for a moment, I caught a fleeting glimpse of them, as one might catch sight of a bit of paper being whirled about in the seething cauldron under a waterfall before it vanished.

I gripped the leg of my chair to avoid being carried away myself. But the gesture came too late. In any case it was a rhetorical gesture. Absurd.

The priest.

Kulka. Nothingness. Leo. Lola said plaintively:

'What about this expedition of yours, Mr Wojtys? In the middle of the night, in the dark? But we shan't be able to see a thing.'

'We certainly shan't be able to see much in the dark,' Fuchs said impatiently and not very politely.

'My wife,' Leo said (he actually said that, with the bird and the bit of wood still hanging down there below). 'My wife,' he said (oh Holy Mother of God), 'my wife' (I clasped my fingers hard) . . . 'but do not let us get excited,' he said cheerfully. 'There's nothing whatever to get excited about, nothing whatever. Everything is in order, we are all sitting here very comfortably, thanks be to God. We are all sitting here on our little sit-upons gratefully enjoying God's gifts, glug, glug, glug, with wine and vodka, and in a short time a little expedition will set out under my guidance to that unique spot where a most marvellous view is to be obtained, thanks, as I was saying, to the marvellous moon dancing tra-la-la in the midst of the mountains, the hills and the vales, tra-la, as I myself saw it twenty-seven years ago minus one month and three days, ladies and gentlemen, when for the first time at the same bewitching hour I went to that remarkable spot and saw. . . .

'Sucking,' he said, and went pale and gasped for breath.

'But's it's getting cloudy,' Lolo said indignantly and rather impolitely. 'It'll be pitch dark and we shan't be able to see a thing.'

'So it's cloudy,' Leo muttered. 'So it's cloudy. That's fine. It was cloudy then too, I remember. I noticed it on the way back, I remember distinctly,' he said impatiently, as if he were in a great hurry. Then he relapsed into thoughtfulness again.

I was thoughtful too. I was thinking all the time, as hard as I could. Kulka, who had withdrawn into the kitchen, reappeared in the doorway.

'Mind your sleeve.'

These words of Leo's made me start. But he was talking to Fuchs, whose sleeve was touching the sauceboat which had contained mayonnaise. Nothing important, take it easy. But why wasn't Louis here, where was he, why wasn't he with her?

The sparrow.

The bit of wood.

The cat.

'My wife doesn't trust me,' Leo announced.

One by one he examined the first three fingers of his right hand, beginning with the forefinger.

'My wife wants to know what I am thinking about, ladies and gentlemen.'

He waved three fingers of his right hand in the air, and I clasped my hands together firmly.

'Ladies and gentlemen, after thirty-seven years of un-blemished married life it is a slight . . . er, disappointment to me that my wife should so nervously enquire what I am thinking about.'

The priest interrupted.

'The cheese, please,' he said. Everyone looked at him, he repeated 'the cheese, please,' Lolo passed him the cheese, but instead of cutting himself a slice he said: 'We might per-haps push the table back a bit, we're rather cramped here.'

'Yes, we might push the table back a bit,' Leo said. 'What was I saying? Oh yes, after all those years of irreproachable, unimpeachable and exemplary married life that was some-thing I felt I did not deserve. After all those years, months, weeks, days, hours, minutes and seconds. Do you realize, ladies and gentlemen, that I sat down with paper and pencil and worked out how many seconds of married life I had enjoyed up to 7.30 this evening? The result, not forgetting to take the leap years into account, was 140,912,984. And since eight o'clock several thousands more have to be added.'

He rose to his feet and sang:

> *If you can't get what you want*
> *You must want what you've got.*

He sat down and grew thoughtful again.

'If you would like to push the table back a little, please do,' he said. 'What was I saying? Oh yes. All those seconds under my wife's and my daughter's eye. Who would ever have supposed that my wife would be suspicious about what I was thinking?'

Again he broke off and grew thoughtful. These repeated relapses into thoughtfulness were untimely, and a strong sense of dismay or disorder or something of the sort became discernible, not perhaps in his speech, but in general, in the whole atmosphere. And this was his celebration. The sparrow. The bit of wood. The cat. It was not about that. So it was about that. But it was not about that. So it was about that.

He was conducting a kind of religious service, and he seemed to be trying to say: See how attentively I am devoting myself to inattention.

Then he went on again.

'So my wife does not trust my thoughts. Tell me, ladies and gentlemen, do I deserve that? It seems to me that I do not. Except that, if we are to tell the truth (yes, do push the table back a bit, I'm cramped too, and these seats are hard, but that can't be helped), except that, as I was saying, if we are to tell the truth, it must be admitted that it is impossible to tell what is going on in someone else's mind. Let me illustrate what I mean. Let us say that I, for example, an exemplary husband and father, pick up this egg-shell.'

He suited the action to the word and went on:

'Supposing I twist it between my fingers like this, quite slowly, in full sight of everybody. It is impossible to imagine anything more innocent, more innocuous, more inoffensive. Nothing but an utterly harmless little pastime, in fact. But let us go a little more closely into the question of how I twist it between my fingers. Because, you see, I can twist it perfectly virtuously and innocently. But, if I want to, I can also . . . Eh? If I want to, I can also twist it in a slightly more . . . Eh? Yes. This is only an example, of course, to show that even the most admirable of husbands might be capable of twisting an egg-shell in his wife's presence in a manner. . . .'

He flushed. He grew purple. It was astonishing. He realized what was happening and half closed his eyes, but made no attempt to dissimulate his shame. On the contrary, he displayed it to everybody like a monstrance.

Still twisting the egg-shell in his fingers, he waited for the flush to pass. Then he opened his eyes again and said:

'Well, that's all, it's nothing.'

The tension relaxed, though in our corner under the lantern they still felt slightly nervous and oppressed. They looked at him, obviously thinking he was a bit off his head. At all events, nobody spoke.

There was a thump from somewhere outside, as if something had fallen. What could it have been? It was a sound apart, an extra, superadded sound, and it engaged my attention and I thought about it for a long time. But I could make nothing of it.

Then Leo quietly and very politely and distinctly said:
'Berg.'
And I, no less politely and distinctly, responded:
'Berg.'

He looked at me briefly and dropped his eyes. We both sat there quietly, listening to the echoes of the word 'berg', as if it were a subterranean monster, one of those that never appear in daylight but was now here, in front of us. They all looked at it, I presume. Suddenly I felt that everything was on the move, like a flood or an avalanche, or an army marching with banners; I felt as if something decisive had happened, and everything was now moving forward in a definite direction. Quick march. Into the breach, dear friends. If Leo alone had said 'berg' it would not have amounted to anything, but I had said it too. My 'berg' coming on top of his had deprived it of its private and confidential character, it was no longer the private expression of a crackpot, but was something that really existed and was here before us, in our presence. It immediately advanced, invaded and took possession.

For a moment I saw the sparrow, the bit of wood, and the cat, and at the same time the mouths also, whirling away and sinking like scraps of paper in a mountain torrent. I was waiting for everything to march off in the berg direction. I was an officer on the general staff, a choir boy helping at mass, an acolyte, the loyal and disciplined servant of a cause. Quick march.

But Lola called out:
'Bravo, Mr Wojtys!'

She ignored me, but I felt certain that she did this for the simple reason that she was afraid, afraid of cooperating with him. The whole thing suddenly collapsed and disintegrated, there was some quiet laughter, everyone started talking, Leo broke into a loud guffaw. It was time for everyone to whet his whistle, ha, ha, ha, ha! How disappointing that such a disastrous collapse should follow such a solemn moment, when everything had been poised for a great leap forward. Once more there was a buzzing as if of a swarm of bees, yes, I'll have a little vodka, aren't you drinking, father? have just a drop of cognac. Jadeczka, Tolo, Lolo, Lola, Fuchs and Lena with that fresh, pretty little mouth of hers, a party on an outing. Everything had collapsed. Nothingness. Once more everything was like a dirty wall. Chaos and confusion.

The sparrow.

The bit of wood.

The cat.

I remembered them just because I was forgetting them. They came back to me because they had been moving away. They were sinking and disappearing. I had to look into myself for the sparrow, the bit of wood and the cat that were sinking and disappearing from sight, I had to look for them, find them and keep them. And I had to make an effort to return in thought to the thicket on the other side of the road and the wall. The priest got up and clumsily extricated himself from between the table and the bench, muttering excuses. He opened the door, and he and his cassock crept out of the room.

In the absence of berg I felt foolish and at a loss. I decided that I too must go outside for a breath of fresh air.

I rose, walked towards the door, and went out.

It was cool on the verandah. The moon. A swelling, towering cloud, solid and luminous. Lower down, and much darker, there was a fountain of petrified mountains. And all round there were fairy-like meadows carpeted with trees and flowers and processions, as in a park where dancing and singing were taking place. The whole was submerged at the bottom of the moonlight.

Near the steps the priest was leaning over the balustrade.

He was motionless, and was doing something strange with his mouth.

X

I SHALL find it difficult to tell the rest of this story. Incidentally, I am not sure that it is one. Such a continual accumulation and disintegration of things can hardly be called a story.

Outside on the verandah, when I saw the priest doing something strange with his mouth, I was taken utterly aback. I should not have been more taken aback if the earth's crust had suddenly burst open and subterranean monsters emerged. Could what I was seeing be true? I alone knew the secret of the mouths. No one but me had been initiated into the mystery of Lena's mouth. It was my secret, and this priest had no right to it. What right had he to put it in his own mouth?

Then I realized that he was vomiting. Yes, vomiting. His wretched, hideous, pitiful vomiting was easy to explain. He had drunk too much.

So much for that. It was insignificant.

He saw me, and produced a shame-faced smile. I was just going to tell him to go to bed and sleep it off when someone else came out on the verandah. It was Jadeczka. She swept past me into the meadow, stopped, put her hand to her mouth, and then by the light of the moon I saw that she was vomiting too.

If the priest vomited, why should she not do the same? Of course. Certainly. But if the priest vomited, that did not excuse her. And her mouth after the priest's mouth. It was like the hanging of the bit of wood than reinforced the hanging of the sparrow, the hanging of the cat that reinforced the hanging of the bit of wood, the knocking that reinforced Kulka's hammering, my berg that reinforced Leo's.

Why did those vomiting mouths grip me like this? What did they know of the mouths concealed inside me? Whence this oral monstrosity? Perhaps the best thing for me to do would be to go away, and I did so. I did not go back into the house, but walked out into the meadow. I had had enough. The night and the moon floating through it were poisoned. There was a halo behind the tops of the trees, and innumerable groupings, processions, conversations, murmurings and whisperings, gay parties and games, were taking place all round. It really was a magical night. I would not go back to them, if I had my way I would never go back to them, probably the thing to do was get into one of the carriages, whip up the horses, and drive away for ever. But no. It was a magnificent night. In spite of everything I was enjoying myself. It was a wonderful night. But I must not prolong it, because I was really ill. It was a wonderful night. No, I was not so ill as all that. The house disappeared behind a hill, and as I approached the stream the turf beneath my feet was very soft. But what was the matter with that tree there, there was something unusual about it.

I stopped. There was a clump of trees, but one of them was different from the others, or rather it was exactly like the others, but there must have been something different about it for it to have attracted my attention. It was concealed by the other trees and it was hard to make it out in the dark, but all the same it somehow attracted my attention —by its unusual density or weight or a sense of strain or something. I walked past it with the feeling that it was terribly heavy, too heavy. I stopped and went back.

I walked into the clump of trees, sure now that there was something there. There were some scattered birches, and then a denser, darker, group of pines. I had a distinct feeling of advancing towards a crushing weight.

I looked round.

A shoe.

A leg hanging from one of the pine-trees. A leg, I said to myself, but was not sure. Another leg. It was a man . . . hanged. I looked again. Yes, it was a man. Legs, shoes, higher up a head all askew. In the darkness of the branches the rest of him was indistinguishable from the tree-trunk.

I looked all round. Nothing, nobody, silence. Then I looked again. A hanged man. There was something familiar about that yellow shoe, it reminded me of Louis's. I moved aside the branches, and saw Louis's jacket and Louis's face.

Louis. Louis, hanging by a belt. His own trouser-belt.

Was it Louis? Yes, it was Louis. I tried to get used to the idea. I could not get used to the idea. If he had hanged himself, he must have had his reasons, and slowly I tried seeking for them and imagining them. Who had hanged him? Had he done it himself? And when had it happened? I remembered that just before supper he had asked me to lend him a razor-blade, he had been quite calm, and during the walk he had seemed perfectly normal. And now, not much more than an hour later, here he was, hanged; and it must somehow have been inevitable, there must have been an accumulation of causes, though I had not the slightest clue to what they might have been. Yet an eddy of which I knew nothing must have disturbed the river that carries everything along, there must have been a blockage of some sort, links and connections and interlocking wheels. But Louis. Why Louis? If it had been Leo, or the priest, or Jadeczka, or even Lena, it would have been less unintelligible. But Louis? Nevertheless here it was, this fact, this hanging fact, the fact of Louis hanged, an enormous, brutal, heavy, aggressive fact, Louis hanging from a pine-tree with his shoes on.

One day I went to the dentist to have a tooth extracted, but for some reason or other the dentist could not grasp it properly with his pincers, which kept slipping, I don't know why, and it was the same with this heavily hanging, inaccessible and ungraspable fact which kept eluding me. If it had happened, in some way or other of course it must have been bound to happen. Cautiously I looked all round. I grew calmer. No doubt because I had understood.

Louis.

The sparrow.

I looked at him exactly as I had looked at the hanged sparrow.

This made four. The sparrow, the bit of wood, the cat, and now Louis. What consistency, what logic. This absurd corpse promptly turned into a rational corpse. But it was a clumsy sort of logic, a rather too personal and private logic of my own.

There was nothing I could do but think, and so I thought. I tried hard to make sense of it. Had he perhaps hanged the sparrow? Had he drawn the arrows, hanged the bit of wood, thought up all those feeble jokes? He must have had a sort of mania, a mania for hanging, which had ended up in his hanging himself here. He must have been mad. I remembered Leo sitting on the tree-trunk and denying, no doubt with complete truthfulness, that he had had anything to do with all that. So it must have been Louis. An obsession, a mania, a kind of madness.

There was also another possibility, this one on the lines of ordinary, normal logic. He might have been the victim of blackmail, someone might have been persecuting him, seeking revenge, perhaps, and might have surrounded him with those warning signs, which might have suggested to him the idea of hanging himself. But who could that have been? A member of the household? Kulka? Leo? Lena? Katasia?

Another, no less 'normal' possibility was that he might not have hanged himself but might have been murdered. Perhaps he had been strangled before being hanged. The maniac who amused himself by hanging things of no significance might have ended by wanting to hang something heavier than the bit of wood. Who might that have been? Leo? Katasia? But Katasia had stayed behind. But what did that prove? She *might* have made her way here secretly, for a thousand reasons and in a thousand ways, there was no limit to the theoretical possibilities. And what about Fuchs? Might he not have succumbed to the hanging contagion? Yes, he might. But he had been with us the whole time. But what of that? If it turned out that it had been he, a gap would certainly be found in his alibi, you could always find anything in the bottomless pit of things that happened. And the priest? There *might* be millions and millions of threads connecting his fat fingers with this hanged man.

It was perfectly conceivable. And what about the peasants who had driven us here? I smiled in the moonlight at the impotence of reason in the face of overflowing, destroying, enveloping reality. Everything was possible and nothing was impossible.

Yes, but the threads were slender, and here was this brutally hanging corpse, fitting so neatly into the sparrow— bit of wood—cat series like a, b, c, d or 1, 2, 3, 4. What consistency, what subterranean logic. It leapt to the eye.

Yet for all its self-evidence it dissolved into nothingness, into a mist, as soon as you tried to include it in the framework of ordinary logic. What arguments Fuchs and I had had. Could one speak of a logical thread connecting the sparrow and the bit of wood, linked as they were by a barely visible arrow on our bedroom ceiling, an arrow so indistinct that we had noticed it only by chance? So indistinct that we had had to complete it in our imagination? Discovering it, and then finding the bit of wood, had been like finding a needle in a haystack. Who, whether Louis or anyone else, would have taken the trouble to devise a whole system of practically invisible clues?

And in any case, what was the connection between the sparrow, the bit of wood and the cat if the cat had been hanged by me? True, the sparrow, the bit of wood and the cat made three hangings, but the third had been done by me, it was I who had added the third rhyme.

The whole thing was illusion, chimaera, moonshine. Yes, but here was this man hanging, and he was the fourth in the series. I wanted to go close and perhaps touch him, but I recoiled. The slight movement I made frightened me, as if it were indecent to move in the presence of a corpse. My horror—for it was horror—derived from the repetition, for the sparrow had been hanging just like this among the trees. I looked all round. What a spectacle. Mountains projecting themselves blindly into the expanse of the sky, on which centaurs, swans, ships, lions with shining manes, were navigating, and below a ballet of hills and woods enveloped in tremulous whiteness. Oh, the moon, a dead sphere shining with borrowed light; its second-hand, weakened, nocturnal glow was as contaminating and poisonous as an illness. And the constellations were unreal, artificial, imposed; they were the obsessions of the luminous sky.

But the important corpse was not the moon's, but Louis's, hanging from a tree just as the cat had been hanging from the wall. One, two, three, four (my counting merged into the distant pulsation of the night). I moved as if to go away, but it was not so easy. The time had not yet come.

What was I to do? The best thing . . . would be to act as if I had seen nothing, let things take their course. Why should I get involved? I was thinking about this when mouths returned to my mind, not very insistently, but they returned: Leo's mouth chewing, the priest's and Jadeczka's mouths vomiting, Katasia's and Lena's mouths, all of them. They imposed themselves on me, not very insistently, but mildly.

I moved my mouth, as if to defend myself, and at the same time the vague thought was at the back of my mind that I must not do that here. In fact what was the point of moving my lips in the presence of this corpse? Doing things in the presence of a corpse is not the same as doing them elsewhere. I felt alarmed and decided to go away.

Simultaneously something else happened that for the past minute I had been afraid was going to happen; I decided that I wanted to look this corpse in the mouth. It was not so much that this thought frightened me as that I more or less guessed that my desire to leave the corpse and go away would make me want to provoke it.

It was that that I was frightened of, and of course it made me want to do it all the more.

But it was not so easy. I should have to move the branches, turn the face towards the moon, look at it. I was not sure whether I should be able to do it without climbing the tree. A complicated and difficult task. Better not touch it.

I touched it, turned the head, looked.

The lips looked blackened, the upper lip was raised and the teeth were visible. A hole, a cavity. For a long time, of course, I had been faced with the possibility, the hypothesis, that one day I should have . . . to hang either myself or her. Hanging had presented itself to me under many aspects, and other theoretical possibilities, many of them very far-fetched, were connected with it. I had already hanged a cat, after all. But a cat is only a cat. Now, for the first time in my life, I was looking human death straight in the mouth. I was looking into a human buccal orifice, the buccal orifice of a hanged man.

Go away and leave it alone.

Go away and leave it alone. It was no business of mine, it had nothing to do with me. I was not under the slightest obligation to find out how or why it had happened. You took a little sand in the hollow of your hand and got hopelessly lost in the infinite, the inconceivable, the immeasurable. How could I hope to discover all the links and connections? He might, for instance, have hanged himself because Lena slept with Leo. How could one tell? One could never tell, one knew nothing. I would go away and leave it alone. But I stayed rooted to the spot, and the thought that passed through my mind was something like: What a pity I've looked him in the mouth, now I shan't be able to go.

This thought surprised me in the brightness of the night, but it was not without good reason. If I had behaved normally with this corpse I should have been able to leave, but after what I had done with my mouth and his mouth I could not. Or rather I could, but if I did I should no longer be able to say that I was not personally involved.

I pondered deeply, very deeply and breathlessly, but without any real thoughts in my mind, and then I started feeling afraid, really afraid, for I was with the corpse and the corpse was with me, and here we were together, and after looking it in the mouth I should not be able to detach myself from it.

I stretched out my hand and put my finger in its mouth.

It was not so easy, the jaws had already begun to stiffen, but I managed to insert my finger and met a strange, unknown tongue and a palate, which struck me as being cold and low, like the ceiling of a low room.

I withdrew my finger and wiped it on my handkerchief.

I looked all round. Had no one seen me? No, no one had seen me. I turned the corpse round into its previous position, concealed it as much as possible behind the branches, obliterated my footprints in the grass, quickly, quickly, I was afraid, my nerves, I was afraid, I must get out of this. I made my way through the clump of trees and, seeing there was nothing but tremulous moonlight, I started walking away. I walked faster and faster in the direction of the house, but I did not run. Then I slowed down. What was I to tell them? How was I to tell them? Things were getting difficult. I had not hanged him. I had not hanged him. But, after putting my finger in his mouth, this hanged man was partly mine.

At the same time I felt a deep satisfaction that at last a link had been established between 'mouth' and 'hanging'. It was I who had done it. At last. I felt as if I had fulfilled my mission.

And now I must go and hang Lena.

I was astonished at this, genuinely astonished, for hitherto the idea of hanging had been purely gratuitous and hypothetical, and after putting my finger in his mouth its nature, so far from changing in any way, had been as eccentric, extravagant or even rhetorical as ever. But the force with which that corpse had entered me and I had entered it had broken down all the barriers. The sparrow had been hanged, and so had the bit of wood and the cat (before it was buried), and so had Louis. Hanged. Hanging and I were one. I stopped and stood still, reflecting that everyone wanted to be himself, and it followed that I too wanted to be myself. Who wanted syphilis, for instance? No one, of course, and yet the syphilitic wanted to be himself, *i.e.*, a syphilitic; it was easy to say he wanted to get well again, but it was like saying 'I don't want to be what I am', it didn't ring true.

The sparrow.

The bit of wood.

The cat.

Louis.

And now I should have to hang Lena.

Her mouth.

Katasia's mouth.

(The priest's and Jadeczka's mouths vomiting).

Louis's mouth.

And now I should have to hang Lena.

Strange. On the one hand, in this remote spot, with the mountains and forests bathed in the moonlight, all this seemed futile, insignificant, unreal, and on the other the tension of the hanging and the tension of the mouths must necessarily lead to. . . . Too bad. It was inevitable.

I walked on with my hands in my pockets.

I reached the top of a slope overlooking the house. I heard the sound of voices and singing. I saw lanterns about half a mile away on a hill opposite. It was they. Leo was showing them the way, and they were keeping up each other's spirits by singing and joking. Lena was with them.

From where I was standing the landscape stretching out before me trembled as if it had been chloroformed. Lena's sudden appearance on the scene had exactly the same effect on me as if I had been out shooting with a double-barrelled shot-gun and had spotted a hare in the distance. I could not help actually laughing. I struck out across country to join them. The sparrow was hanging and on I went. The bit of wood was hanging and on I went. I had hanged the cat and on I went. Louis was hanging and on I went.

I caught up with them just when they were leaving a barely visible path and going down into a wood. There was a lot of undergrowth and sharp stones, and they were advancing cautiously, and Leo, carrying a lantern, was acting as guide. They were joking and calling out to one another. 'Guide us, guide!' they shouted or 'why are we going down instead of up?' Somebody wanted to know how there could be a magnificent view right at the bottom of a dip, and somebody else announced a determination to sit down and not walk another step.

'Patience, patience,' said Leo, 'we haven't got far to go now, we'll soon be there, keep behind me, it's not much farther now.'

They had not noticed me, and I followed them. Lena was walking slightly apart from the others, and there would have been no difficulty in approaching her. I approached her in my role of strangler and hangman, and it would not have been difficult to take her aside (for we were in love, she was just as much in love with me as I was with her, there could be no doubt about that, because if I wanted to kill her it followed that she must be in love with me). And if I took her aside it would be easy to strangle her and hang her. I started realizing what it is like to be a murderer. You murder when murder is easy, when there is nothing else for you to do; the other possibilities have merely been exhausted. The sparrow was hanging, the bit of wood was hanging, Louis was hanging, and I was going to hang her as I had hanged the cat. Of course I might not hang her, but what a let-down, what a fiasco, that would be. Was I to disturb the natural order of things? After all that striving and scheming hanging had been plainly revealed to me and I had connected it with 'mouth'. Was I to give up and become a renegade now?

Out of the question.

I followed them. They played with their lanterns. Sometimes at the cinema you see a comic sequence in which a hunter cautiously advances with his gun at the ready while just behind him, following in his tracks, a fearsome wild beast, a huge bear or gigantic gorilla, is stalking him. The wild beast stalking me in this instance was the priest. He was walking close behind me and a little to one side, and obviously he was trailing in the rear without knowing where he was going or why. Perhaps he had been afraid of being left alone in the house. At first I had not noticed him, and I had no idea how long he had been at my heels with those big, peasant fingers of his which he kept fidgeting. And in his cassock. Heaven and hell. Sin. Our mother, the Holy Catholic Church. The cold of the confessional. The Church and the Pope. Damnation. The cassock. Heaven and hell. *Ite missa est.* Sin. Virtue. The cold of the confessional. *Sequentia sancti.* . . . The Church. Hell. The cassock. Sin. The cold of the confessional.

I gave him a violent push that made him stagger. Terror overcame me as I did so. What on earth had come over me? Had I gone mad? Now he would make a scene.

He did not. My hand met such a pathetic passivity that I felt totally reassured. He stood still without even looking at me. We stayed like that. I could see his face plainly. And his mouth. I raised my hand, wanting to stick a finger in his mouth, but he was gritting his teeth. I took his chin in my left hand, opened his mouth, and put my finger in.

I withdrew it and wiped it with my handkerchief.

I had to hasten my stride to catch up with the others. Sticking my finger in this priest's mouth had done me good, it was quite different from doing it to a corpse, and it was like introducing my chimaeras into the real world. I felt bolder and more cheerful. It struck me that all this had momentarily distracted me from the sparrow, etc., so I resumed awareness of the fact that down below some twenty-five miles away it was still there, with the bit of wood and the cat. Katasia was there too.

'Ladies and gentlemen,' Leo announced, 'let us pause here for a short rest.'

He was standing under a huge rock overhanging a gully rank with vegetation. Immediately in front of the rock there was a small clearing; it must have been a much frequented place, I thought I could make out wheel-tracks. There were some bushes and some grass. 'Lolo, I don't like it here, what a funny place he has chosen.' 'But colonel, there isn't anywhere to sit down.' 'My dear president, are we to sit on the bare earth?'

'All right, all right,' said Leo plaintively. 'But papa has lost a button from his sleeve. Ye gods, a button. Won't somebody bring a lantern?'

The sparrow.

The bit of wood.

The cat.

Louis.

The priest.

Leo bent up double looking for his button while Lolo held the lantern for him. I remembered Katasia's room, and Fuchs and me searching it with a pocket lamp. How long ago that had been. The room was still there, and so was Katasia. He went on searching, and ended by taking the lantern from Lolo's hands. But soon I noticed that, instead of using it to illuminate the ground, he was surreptitiously shining it on the big rock and other rocks that were lying around, reminding me of the way the pocket torch had flitted about when Fuchs and I examined the walls of Katasia's room. Was he really looking for a lost button? Perhaps he was doing nothing of the sort, perhaps this was the place to which he had been leading us, the place where twenty-seven years before . . . but he was not sure. He could not recognize it for certain. Since then new trees had grown, the ground had sunk, the rock might have shifted. He searched more and more feverishly, just as we had done. Seeing him wavering thus, lost and uncertain, almost drowning, with the water up to his chin, I could not help remembering how lost Fuchs and I had been in those ceilings, walls, and flower-

163

beds. But that was the past. Meanwhile everybody waited and nobody spoke, perhaps because everyone was curious to see what was going to happen. I caught sight of Lena. She was delicate, like lace, and she was there with the sparrow, the cat, Katasia, Louis and the priest.

Leo was lost, bewildered and at his wit's end. He leaned over and examined the base of the rock. Silence.

Then he stood erect again.

'It's here,' he announced.

'But what is here, Mr Wojtys?' Lola said plaintively. 'We can't see anything.'

Leo faced us modestly, calmly and confidently.

'What an amazing coincidence, my friends,' he said. 'What a truly amazing coincidence. The odds against must have been about a million to one. Here was I looking for a shirt button when I realized that this rock . . . that I had been here before. It was here that I, twenty-seven years ago . . . it was here.'

He relapsed into thoughtfulness as suddenly if on a word of command, and remained like that. This went on and on. No one moved or spoke, and not till several minutes had passed did Lola say quietly and anxiously:

'What is the matter with you, Mr Wojtys?'

'Nothing,' he replied.

I noticed that Kulka was not present. Had she been left behind? Had she hanged Louis, perhaps? What nonsense, he had hanged himself. Why? Nobody knew yet. What would happen when they found out?

The sparrow.

The bit of wood.

The cat.

Louis.

It was exceedingly difficult to realize that what was happening here and now was related to other things that had happened in that house more than twenty miles away. I resented the fact that Leo was playing first violin and that everyone (myself included) had turned into an audience for him. We had been brought here to. . . .

He indistinctly muttered:

'Here. With a. . . .'

Several more minutes passed in silence. They were long minutes that reeked of lewdness, but they had their own eloquence, for if nobody spoke it meant that we were here for the sole purpose of enabling him to obtain his satisfaction in our presence. 'One is what one is.' We waited for him to finish. Time passed.

Suddenly he shone the lantern on his own face. His pince-nez, his bald pate, his mouth, everything. His eyes were shut. Voluptuary and martyr. Then he said: 'That's all there is to see,' and put out the lantern.

The darkness leapt at me, it was much darker than one would have expected, clouds must have gathered overhead. Under the great rock he was almost invisible. What was he doing? He must have been surrendering to I don't know what lewd thoughts, concentrating on the memory of that one and only woman of his, celebrating his own lubricity. But . . . supposing he were not absolutely sure that this was the right spot? Supposing he had just picked on it at random?

I was surprised to see that nobody moved, though they must all have realized why they had been brought here—to be in attendance on him, look at him, excite him by watching him. It would have been so easy to get up and go, but nobody moved. Lena, for instance, could have gone, but did not. She did not move. He began panting rhythmically. No one could see what he was doing, but he did not move. He groaned. He groaned aloud. It was a licentious groan but also a laborious one, to increase his lubricity. He groaned and whimpered. It was a stifled, guttural whimper. How he worked at it, struggled and strained, concentrated and celebrated. He worked and we waited. Then he said:

'Berg.'

'Berg,' I replied.

'Bamberging in the berg,' he shouted, and I replied:

'Bamberging in the berg.'

He quietened down completely and total silence prevailed. I thought sparrow Lena bit of wood cat in the mouth honey disfigured lip little clump of earth tear in the wallpaper finger Louis young trees hanging Lena lonely there teapot cat bit of wood fence road Louis priest wall cat bit of wood sparrow

165

cat Louis hanged bit of wood hanged sparrow hanged Louis cat I'm going to hang. . . .

Suddenly it started raining. First big, isolated drops made us raise our heads, and then the heavens opened. A wind arose, universal panic broke out, everyone dashed for shelter to the nearest tree. But the big pines offered no protection, they dripped and dripped, water, water, everywhere, wet hair, wet shoulders, wet thighs, facing us in the darkness a vertical wall of water penetrated only by the pathetic light of the lanterns, by the light of which I saw rain falling and water flowing, forming rivulets and waterfalls and lakes, pouring and splashing everywhere, with gurgling torrents in which leaves and bits of straw or wood were carried away and disappeared. Torrents united into rivers, islands and blockages and obstacles appeared, streams flowed round them in complicated patterns, above the deluge continued and below a leaf was carried away or a bit of bark vanished in the flood. It all ended up in shivers and colds and fever. Lena had tonsillitis, and a taxi had to be sent for from Zakopane. Illness, doctors, in short everything changed.

I went back to Warsaw and my parents—warfare with my father was resumed—and to other things, problems, difficulties and complications. Today we had chicken and rice for lunch.

THE END